I'd Like

I'd Like

Amanda Michalopoulou

Translation from the Greek by Karen Emmerich

DALKEY ARCHIVE PRESS
Champaign & London

Originally published in Greek as *Tha ithela* by Kastaniotis, 2005

First English translation, 2008

Library of Congress Cataloging-in-Publication Data

Michalopoulou, Amanta, 1966-
[Tha ethela. English]
I'd like / Amanda Michalopoulou ; translation by Karen Emmerich.
p. cm.
ISBN-13: 978-1-56478-493-3 (alk. paper)
ISBN-10: 1-56478-493-2 (alk. paper)
1. Short stories, Greek (Modern) 2. Greek fiction, Modern. I. Emmerich, Karen. II. Title.
PA5624.I27T4913 2008
889.3'0108--dc22

2007040803

The present edition of *I'd Like* was co-financed by the National Endowment for the Arts, a federal agency, and the National Book Centre of Greece; support was also provided by a grant from the Illinois Arts Council, a state agency, and by the University of Illinois at Urbana-Champaign.

www.dalkeyarchive.com

Designed by Jack Henrie Fisher
Printed on permanent/durable acid-free paper and bound in the United States of America

To my parents

Contents

I'd Like

"Now! He's alone!"

Vandoros is standing across the room from us, scratching his reddish beard. With his leather gloves and penetrating gaze he looks just like a fox.

"What are you waiting for?" I hiss.

My husband loosens his bow tie and crosses the room in his characteristic bouncing gait. He'd come up to me just like that, years ago, at a movie theater in Athens. "Don't tell me you liked that film," he'd said then. No, but I had liked his peculiar blend of awkwardness and chivalry.

A waiter steps into his path, holding out a tray bearing a solitary glass of wine. My husband drinks it down in a single swallow, then looks at me and shrugs. The window of opportunity has closed. Vandoros is no longer alone. An older man with glasses is clapping him on the back as if they're old friends.

I go over, carrying my own drink, a glass of pink champagne.

"You think that's his father? Or do famous people come straight from God?"

He loosens his tie even more, then takes it off and stuffs it in his pocket.

"For Christ's sake! Did he really have to offer me a drink at that precise moment?"

"Did you really have to take it?"

The room has filled up. Men, women, and a few children whose parents must have dragged them there are perched on the edges of their seats, chatting or glancing out the windows, which rattle each time a bus passes by. Night has started to fall. Summer presses in from all sides, thick and sticky.

"Lots of journalists came."

He twirls the empty glass in his hand, covering it with fingerprints.

"Of course they did. It's an easy story, a sure thing," I whisper.

We set our bags down in the fifth row from the front, on the left, in the exact spot where writers look when they get nervous. My husband insists there's a particular place, which he calls a "distraction spot." Whenever he gives a reading he always throws sideways glances at that spot, searching for comfort and acceptance.

Tonight the room is brimming with acceptance. Vandoros has had more success with two novels than my husband has with seven. Everyone's talking about his strong, sturdy Greece, which emerges out of the past "with courage and clamor," as the title of his first book has it. They're talking about him, too: a second-generation Greek-American with a wrinkled crease in his linen pants and a cigarette always dangling from one hand.

"There's his wife!"

"Where?"

"Don't be catty. She's not *that* short."

But I actually hadn't seen her. I wasn't looking at anything in particular; I was in my own distraction spot, right there in my seat, swimming in a bog of elbows, knees, and plastic bags from bookstores. His wife belongs to that category of women who pass unnoticed, whose presence a room simply absorbs—until, that is, they open their mouths, gesturing vividly to give life and color to whatever point they're trying to make. Then she surfaces, shaking off her diminutive stature, her pale skin, the circles under her eyes. Her name is Pia Saunders. She's several years younger than I am, and takes part in all the contemporary art biennials.

My husband and I would never admit it to one another, but we both imagine them in the exotic locales where the biennials are held—Korea, Cuba, Brazil. Drinking cocktails at the hotel bar, half-slices of pineapple stuck on the rims of their glasses, then going back to their room drunk on happiness. And on a particular kind of happiness, the kind that circumstances provide. They don't need to look at the world through new eyes; the world has changed for their benefit: deserts and dug-out canoes instead of apartment buildings and turnpike tolls. He writes on the hotel balcony—standing up, he says in interviews, like Nabokov. He gazes out at the lights of each new, exotic city trembling in the distance, and thinks of Greece, which he imagines as a tranquil, mythical sheep. She takes photographs and gives them titles like *Our Little Secret* or *A Few Things I'd Like to Show You.*

She's thrown a white shawl over her elegant dress—a white tunic with pleats that end at her ankles. She's massaging her temples and yawning. *The evil eye,* Vandoros writes in his new novel, *is the fleeting but deep desire to step into the other's shoes, to sleep between his sheets, if possible with his wife.*

I wouldn't want to sleep with Vandoros. But it would be a relief to me if he could read my mind and say, *I understand, it's human, I used to think that way, too.* I'd like for the four of us to go out for drinks after the reading, to talk about these kinds of things. At the end of the night they would invite us to come and visit them in New York, where Saunders would carry an armful of sheets into the guestroom, and linger so long, postponing the final goodnight, that in the end I would take the sheets from her arms and say, *Come on, Pia, tomorrow's another day.*

"What are you thinking?"

"Nothing."

And it's true, they aren't really thoughts. They're little shouts that never make it out, stray cries that form a halo around my head, as if to adorn some imminent, dramatic gesture of utter defeat.

Unfortunately. If only. Because.

Impossible.

I'd like.

Vandoros climbs the steps to the podium, hunched over. He has nothing to prove; he doesn't have to try to look like anyone but himself.

"What are *you* thinking?"

"Me? Nothing."

I know him. He thinks like I do, only in a more masculine way: without words. He'd like to melt into his chair as Vandoros clears his throat and says, in broken Greek, "Thank you for coming. Good evening."

"He's going to read with his gloves on? Is he crazy?"

"Maybe he has contact dermatitis."

"From writing too much?"

"Don't exaggerate. Look, he won't even take them off to shake hands with Stark."

The woman introducing him is an American philhellene with a double chin who has translated Cavafy. My husband crosses and uncrosses his legs. He slips his hand into the pocket with his bow tie. He sent her a book of his once, but never got a response.

"Today we are honored . . ." Stark is saying. And honor assumes its pious form. The women's heads turn like flowers turning to the sun, the men lean back with their legs apart as if they were sitting in the coffee house waiting for the mayor to start speaking in his own words about their lives. The waves of their presence wash over us as over a broken seawall.

My husband grips my hand in his, hard. Both of us hear the snapping of bone, but only I feel the pain. No one can follow me that far, that deep.

Something is out of joint.

The emergency room smells like ammonia. Maybe things are so busy that the young doctor doesn't have time to go to the men's room, and just relieves himself in the corner. We wait for almost two hours, with teenagers who fell off their motorbikes, a woman who burned her hand on the stove, and a man who cracked his head falling drunk out of bed. I stare entranced at my little finger, which has separated from my palm and is pointing toward something just beyond my field of vision. Then a gurney passes in front of us and I stop thinking about myself. Face and body covered with a sheet. The only thing showing is a wisp of reddish hair. There's a red beret lying on top of the sheet, as if the girl is just taking a little nap and will sit up any minute and put it back on. The men pushing the stretcher walk off in search of the head nurse. I reach out, grab the beret, and stuff it in my bag.

Eventually they show me into one of the semi-private examining rooms, where I sit with one leg hanging on either side of the leather examining table, left and right, like an inmate in an asylum who thinks she's a knight. A crumpled length of paper, stained with a little blood from the previous patient, rustles against my thigh, absorbing my sweat. My husband has turned the x-ray into a fan. The crinkling of the plastic reminds me of the grinding of bone on bone.

"Your face is all yellow, you know."

He's pulled his bow tie from his pocket and is playing with it again.

"And you're bright red."

"It's stuffy in here."

We smile tiredly. The doctor gives me an injection of painkillers and prepares a splint for my finger. Then the head nurse pages him over the loudspeaker. He excuses himself and disappears. We're left alone again with our thoughts, which swim around us, drowning in the heat.

Suddenly the door swings open and a face appears. The face belongs to the absolute last person I would've expected to see here: Pia Saunders, in a wheelchair, her shawl draped over her knees. A nurse is pushing the wheelchair into the room. I look down; Saunders's left ankle is as swollen and red as a half-eaten blood orange. Vandoros follows behind. He tells us that his wife's shoe got caught in the hem of her dress, and explains what happened afterward. Saunders is biting her bottom lip and grimacing. The doctor comes into the room and closes the door, smiling conspiratorially.

"If the crowd out there lynches me, Mr. Vandoros, the crime will be on your head."

Then he turns to us.

"Would you mind waiting just a few more minutes? This gentleman is a well-known writer, and a member of the Greek diaspora.

We should show him that Greek hospitality is still alive and well, shouldn't we?"

With my good hand I make a vague gesture in the air, like a conductor.

"Can you believe it?" I hiss to my husband. "They cut ahead of us. It makes me want to . . ."

"What?"

"Punch him in the face."

"Shhh!" my husband hisses. "Enough already."

We stare out the window like two punished children.

"Do you mind if we open the window a little?" I ask. "It's awfully hot in here."

Vandoros walks toward us. The crease in his linen pants is entirely gone, and the fabric flutters gently as he moves. His jacket flutters too, his crumpled gloves peeking out of one pocket. He uses his handkerchief to turn the handle, and the window creaks open. There's a metal instrument box on the windowsill, in which the doctor's cigarette butts lay drowned in a half-inch of water. Vandoros winks at us and lights a cigarette of his own.

"Weren't you two at the . . ."

"Yes," my husband says, his face lighting up. So the distraction spot really does exist. "Our accident happened before you even started reading, so we missed—"

"Please. You didn't miss a thing," Vandoros cuts in. "What happened to your wife?"

My husband offers a slightly edited version of the actual accident. Vandoros sticks his arm with the cigarette out the window, a gesture presumably intended to demonstrate his regard for the hospital's rules.

"I needed that," he says.

The smoke from his cigarette whirls and dissipates in the darkness.

"It helps," my husband agrees. My husband never smokes.

"Can I offer you one?"

My husband puts down his bow tie and takes the cigarette.

"A light? The only thing I can't offer you is a good pair of lungs to smoke it with; mine are completely destroyed."

My husband bends down to light his cigarette. He blows the smoke out the window, awkwardly, but with relief.

In their suite at the Grande Bretagne, Saunders is wearing a silk robe painted with almond blossoms. She's stretched out like an odalisque on the bed, half reclining, scratching the sole of her bandaged foot. Her toes are bright red from the pressure of the bandage.

"God, it itches like crazy."

She rolls over onto her back, her body sinking into the thick down comforter. Our husbands are drinking whiskey on the balcony. The darkness, deeper just around the outline of their bodies, moves with them as they gesture.

"Come here," she says, patting the bed beside her as if I were a dog.

I climb up next to her and we tell one another how much pain we're in. Saunders is drinking white wine, I'm drinking vodka with a splash of orange juice. I accidentally touch the silk belt of her robe. The way she's dressed makes her look even kinder and more innocent than before.

"I like you, but I can't just play dumb," I say.

"What do you mean?"

"If we hadn't both gotten hurt, we wouldn't be here right now."

"I still don't understand."

A little tipsy from the champagne, the vodka, and the anti-inflammatory the doctor prescribed, I explain to her how artists feel when they meet other artists who have achieved something tangible, something everyone can recognize, even those who think art is a waste of time. Saunders shakes her head, blinks her moist, black eyes, and gives me a little lecture on the relativity of goals. She is compassionate and well-meaning because she is self-sufficient.

"You'll have to show me your work. What do you paint?"

I explain, offering all kinds of details that won't really help her understand. My sentences all hang unfinished in the air.

"I just don't know what I'm doing anymore, where I am."

"Relax, you'll figure it out."

If your position in the world really depends that much on your point of view, then what she says works like a charm: I let my head drop back and examine the room upside-down. I haven't felt this way in a long time. A wave of optimism, the belief that life can change. Then, with a shudder, my old self returns.

"I don't want to do anything anymore. Just to watch."

"What do you mean?"

"I just want to watch while other people make art. And be jealous. I like thinking I've missed the boat."

"Fine, if melodrama makes you more productive."

"Sure, but it can be dangerous, too. You start to believe you're a nobody, and that makes you want to give up altogether."

"It's not that simple. When you choose something, it chooses you, too."

"You mean it's too late, there's no going back? That would be nice."

We fall silent, wrapped in the air conditioning's artificial cool and the lingering odor of freshly painted walls.

"I don't think I agree with you," she says after a while. "Conversations about art are so boring. Not boring, just silly. You end up talking about a work of art as if it were a cake in a bakery window. The misguided notion that art is something separate from other pursuits disappears when you put things in their proper order. I mean, here we are, bandaged, lying in bed, talking about painting the same way we would say, Isn't life crazy, or, I need a lover, or, What do you feel like eating? And our husbands, the ones responsible for all this, are out there downing whiskey like water. I'm sure they're enjoying this whole debacle."

"Responsible? But it was a mistake! I twisted my little finger inwards, it's a nervous habit, I dig the nail of my little finger into my palm, and—"

Suddenly I understand the significance of the plural: *our husbands.* I sit up carefully so as not to startle her.

"You mean he pushed you?"

"He hates the obligatory dinners they always have after these readings. All the people who come up and shake his hand, congratulate him, tell him they read his book." She drains the last drops of wine from her glass. "Besides, he's afraid of germs."

"So that's why he used his handkerchief to open the window? And the gloves . . ."

“He’d rather die than shake someone’s hand. They told us there was going to be a dinner in our honor and . . .”

“He pushed you to get out of it?”

“He likes to push.”

“You mean his stories . . . The dogs that rape the café owner, the teacher who pours hot oil on her students, the priest and his wife who set traps in the stable . . .”

“Well, he’s certainly never set traps. He’s impulsive and has a quick temper. Don’t even get me started on his childhood. But he’s still my husband.”

We’re lying face-up on the bed. If we leaned our heads back, we would see our husbands hanging from the balcony like bats.

I’ve probably had enough to drink.

“He told me he feels there’s a kinship between us.”’

He’s driving with his shirt unbuttoned. The morning air rushing in through the open windows rustles the hair on his chest.

“A kinship?”

“A literary one.”

“Are you crazy? His books are unreadable.”

“You’re wrong. He’s satirizing himself. He said that, at the end of a reading, everyone always comes up and wants to talk to him. That’s how he knows he hasn’t yet written the thing that will make people uncomfortable, that will make them realize some shocking truth about themselves. If he had, they wouldn’t smile those stupid smiles, munching on crackers at the reception. They would avoid him.”

“Well, that would suit him just fine. Pia told me he’s terrified of germs.”

“Now are you sorry you made fun of him for wearing those gloves?”

“If you ask me, he makes a big deal even out of his weaknesses.”

“Don’t be so negative. He invited us for a drink tomorrow. This could lead somewhere.”

“Yeah, to another drunken night.”

“I’m not drunk. He seemed like a good guy. I expected him to be a pompous fool, but he turned out to be a regular guy.”

“Regular?”

Regularity is the way the dotted lines follow one another on the asphalt. Regularity is the traffic lights changing from red to green, stop to go. Regularity is having a job that gets you out of bed every morning and shuts the valve in your brain, keeps you from thinking. Regularity is living in a vast factory full of noises that tell you do this, do that, take a break, eat something, go to sleep, and when no one's looking, cry a little, if you like. It's past six on a Wednesday morning and we're headed home to take two aspirin and put ourselves to bed. We're headed home to feel useless again.

"He beats her. That's his secret, that he beats her."

My husband is practicing smoking by the open balcony door. I'm sitting at my dressing table, brushing my hair and watching him in the mirror. He turns toward me abruptly and the ash from his cigarette drops to the floor.

"What do you mean?"

"Exactly what I said. He *beats* her. And apparently tries to atone for it in his writing."

He takes a deep drag on his cigarette. I'm excited by his mimicry, his resignation, his gullibility. His wide stride.

"Aren't you going to say anything? I feel like hitting you myself!"

I smack the hairbrush against my open palm to show him how. My elbow flies out and sweeps a little ornamental cat off the dressing table and onto the floor. That cat has been sitting there for as long as I can remember, holding down the phone and electric bills, playing with its ball of yarn. But now it takes everything down with it, the bills, the yarn, and smashes into a thousand pieces on the floor.

"Just because my ash fell on the floor?"

I pick up the shattered pieces of the cat.

"No, because you're always asking the wrong questions!"

"What do you want me to ask? How exactly he beats her? If he pushes her down and kicks her? Is that what you want? To gossip?"

"I want to feel your surprise. You know why your stories have become so hollow? Your characters hear the strangest things in the world and just go on eating their cake. Or smoking."

"Thanks for the constructive criticism! That's just what I need at six in the morning!"

My finger burns inside its splint.

"Why don't we continue this conversation in the morning?" my husband says.

"It is morning."

"All of a sudden I'm exhausted."

"You're always exhausted, every time anything happens to upset the status quo. Just don't take up smoking, please. We've got enough to deal with already, what with the drinking and the constant fault-finding."

He closes the shutters and night falls again, just for the two of us. His exhaustion is contagious. First my brain goes numb, then my hands, then my knees. How will I ever find the strength to take off my clothes and slip into bed? It seems like the most difficult thing in the world. So I just watch him undress.

First his shirt. Then his shoes. He pulls his socks off together with his pants.

A failed writer in boxer shorts.

A failed painter, fully dressed.

We don't hit each other. And we don't embrace.

There are other ways.

We're awoken by the shrieking of an ambulance's siren. It turns out to be the telephone. My voice, sober, serious, and slightly deeper than it really is, says, "Please leave a message after the beep."

"Good morning, it's Vandoros calling. We were thinking you might like to come for brunch. We've got way too many croissants and marmalade, all these animals in thin slices, and we really don't know what to do with them."

"What's he talking about?" my husband groans.

"Brunch. He wants us to come for brunch."

He makes a movement, as if he were about to punch me in the eye. Does he want to make up after yesterday? I prefer to drink my coffee alone and maintain my haughty air—the closer it gets to melancholy, the more it drags me into its depths.

"Are you going to pout like that all day?"

I push open the shutters and am blinded by the light. Nothing outside is moving, not even the heat. How would I translate that into paint? A sweating canvas.

"How's your hand?"

"Better."

"So what's wrong?"

I think about how other people have real problems. Where to leave their kids while they go and sign some contract. When they'll be able to visit their sick mother. What to wear and what to say at a funeral, or a wedding. The two of us live at a safe distance from our relatives, and from the rest of society for that matter. Our sadness is as viscous and unmoving as the heat. Success, competition, the subjects of our art have replaced daily worries, family, the meaning of life.

"Nothing. My head hurts, that's all."

Sometimes the headaches come when nothing else does—a genuine, catastrophic pain. There's something ironic about my finger getting crushed. It's my pinky finger, after all. I don't actually need it to paint or eat.

"You want a massage?"

His fingers knead the base of my neck impatiently, pulling the roots of my hair.

"You're hurting me!"

"Sorry."

"Do you think they'd take any interest in us if circumstances were different?"

"What do you mean, different?"

"If you'd gone up to congratulate him after his reading, for instance."

"How should I know? You're always asking hypothetical questions."

"I'm kind of obsessed with them, that's all."

"But you're treating them like a moving metaphor, not like actual people."

"So did you, until you suddenly pushed your way into the friend category."

"He called, not me."

"Sure, but only because you said what he wanted to hear."

"Are we going to brunch or not?"

"I'm not. You go if you want."

He closes the door behind him nonchalantly, as if it's perfectly natural for him to be going somewhere without me. I throw some water on my face and sit down in front of a canvas whose colors I've changed at least a half-dozen times. It shows a knight riding backwards, grasping his horse's tail. At first the knight was white. Then he acquired a gray beard, a red face, a black cape, and the bright yellow wings of a fly. I have no idea what longing produced that knight. I'm afraid it might have been the longing for longing. At first art is like eros—fragile, pleasantly painful. It follows the rhythm of your breathing, the movement of your hands. Then you get used to it. It becomes a necessary endeavor. When I don't know what I want to paint I get annoyed, as if that ambivalence were something unnatural.

The ringing of the phone startles me and my hand slips, mistakenly throwing a patch of red into the air beside the knight's arm.

"It's Pia. Pick up. Why didn't you come?"

Why would I? Were they expecting me to entertain them again with another monologue of desolation and despair?

"Come on, pick up. I know you're there!"

Then there's a sigh and the answering machine's monotonous hum.

I go into the bathroom and brush my teeth to get rid of the acrid taste of sleep, my disappointment, the whole noontime itself. The phone rings again.

"It's Pia again. If you don't come, we're going to pack up all the jam and bring it to you."

"Tell her there are croissants, too," my husband calls from inside.

I lock up the studio. I throw on a jacket over my checked skirt and grab my purse. They're after me, I have to get away, get away. As far as I can.

A man is pulling my hair. Playfully at first, then harder. "Stop!" I shout, and am awoken by the sound of my own voice. I sit up on the bench, shoving my hands between my thighs to warm them. I must have dozed off. Now I feel vulnerable—not so much because of the nightmare as because of this sudden return to reality.

I'm sitting on a bench behind Notre Dame. The clouds are sinking lower and lower in the sky; any minute now they'll be touching the top of my head. The breeze blows a lock of hair into my mouth, another into my nostrils, but I'm too cold to take my hands out of the little pouch I've made for them in my skirt. I fish the red beret out of my purse and pull it down over my ears. September in Paris isn't at all like September in Athens. No humid heat, no sweat. Just a freezing wind.

How did I end up here? I walked hypnotized into the departures hall at the airport and read the list of departing flights as if it were the menu of daily specials at a restaurant. Paris, or rack of lamb? I'll have the Paris, please, and a glass of white wine.

It's not something I do often. I'm neither rich nor impulsive. But when I pictured them descending on the apartment with their croissants, it occurred to me that we're living a life of substitutes. That somewhere there's a core of original life, a place where things don't just resemble other things. Croissants, for instance. That silly, romantic notion started it all.

When we were first married, my husband and I used to go to Paris hoping to run into the ghosts of Miró and Gertrude Stein. Some of his stories had been translated into French, for anthologies of Greek fiction, and my work had been included in a few group exhibitions. Very large groups: thirty Greeks, an entire platoon, would fly together to Paris for a few days. As soon as we arrived, our moveable feast would disperse like the bubbles in a glass of champagne. A moveable feast—that's what Hemingway called the Paris of his day, when Fitzgerald and Pound were living there, too. Now I see clearly that our own feast was entirely stationary.

Only the children give movement to the frozen landscape before me, with the bristling cathedral that pricks me all over with its towers and pediments. The children appeared out of nowhere, chasing one another in their colorful windbreakers, spreading their arms wide, pretending they're planes. Their nanny is eating a puff pastry topped with big crystals of sugar. Why didn't we ever have kids? Would they have distracted us from our lofty ambitions?

"Careful!" the nanny calls, and I wonder if she's talking to me.

I am careful, I want to tell her. So careful I no longer know how to paint, or whether I'll paint to the bitter end. Maybe it would be better to die of frostbite on this bench behind Notre Dame, in my jacket and my secondhand beret, like those homeless women who bring food for the pigeons.

Just listen to me and don't say a word or I'll hang up. I'm in Paris. I have a fever. I fainted in the Louvre and they had to carry me back to my hotel. I wanted to see all the artworks in the museum once. Those works that once surprised me. That frightened me. That convinced me I needed to paint.

Do you remember how insatiably I used to paint? I devoured the paper, chewed on my brushes. My feet never hurt in museums—I forgot they even existed. I could live for days on a single croissant; I believed that time and despair would never touch me. Can you tell me why art drives a person crazy when it promises so much? We should've known that things would end up here. In a room in the same hotel, twenty years later. The same rococo table, the blue checked bedspreads and the basket of apples from the management, with peels so many different shades of red they look painted. Why do we say that, anyway, that something real looks painted? Why do people assume that art corrects the failings of life?

I'm afraid of dying in the most ridiculous way possible. Of pneumonia and nostalgia, like your favorite poets who all dropped like flies in sanatoria in the days before penicillin. I have that knitted beret with me, too. It'll be the perfect finishing touch. If you were here, I might change my mind. If you held my hand and told me that things would be different. That we'd come to live in the south of France, where the sunlight has healed all kinds of painters, and their paintings, too. I would do little aquarelles, and you would write stories, and at night we would listen to the crickets chirp. We wouldn't know anyone, and no one would know us. Only the baker. And the man at the wine shop. Yes, but we'd still wake up at noon and when I'd ask you to rub my neck you wouldn't do it with true self-sacrifice, as you used to. As I'd like you to.

"I'd like." How stupid, how overly refined and polite—so many trampled wishes in two little words. If I really wanted them to come true, I would have used the simple, concise verb "want." The favorite verb of children everywhere. You know what I'd like? To accept the idea that longing simply exists. Like clothes. Hands. Hair. You touch them, they touch you, and that's that.

I'd like for you to follow my train of thought until you find me.

Fast, if you can.

Now.

"Are you crazy?"

Your voice emerges from a labyrinth of dizzying turns; the vowels rush blindly forward and burst, but the consonants are slow in finding their way. A distorted voice, a tender voice. Precisely as I'd have liked it to be.

"When did you get here?"

"A little while ago. How are you feeling?"

"Better."

"Your finger?"

"It's better, too."

Now the other fingers on that hand hurt, too. All of my fingers and toes, in fact. My knees, my ankles, my elbows. The nape of my neck, my thighs, my eyelids. Whatever opens, closes, moves.

"Are you going to tell me why you did this?"

"We can't live the way we were living."

"Forget the fancy phrases. Are you sick of me?"

"I don't mean between us. I mean each of us with ourselves."

"Those two things are related."

"Sure, down the road."

You pull your chair closer to the bed and take my hand gently—very gently, by your standards, as if you're afraid you might break it again.

"Pia and Vandoros send their love."

"One evening and they love me already?"

"It's an expression."

"Do you still find them fascinating?"

"I find them real. Problematic and insecure."

"And me, do you think I'm petty?"

"Impulsive. You call him that, but you're worse. You know, it would have suited you to live here, in Paris, at the height of surrealism. With a fur that ended in little raccoon paws. And all day you would . . ."

Your hand stops drawing the fur in the air and drops into your lap. The whole room holds its breath. The blue checked bedspreads gape. Their tassels are motionless, the apples are like black holes, and behind the curtains lies a still, bruised sky.

"Could you bring me some water, please?"

I like the sight of you moving through the room, touching things, taking care of me. My water, the bubbles, it all makes me happy. One of the joys of being sick is experiencing other people's self-sacrifice.

"Look . . ."

You open the curtains and a dark cloud practically bursts into the room. Gray and wrinkled, like an elephant's ear.

"Is it raining?"

"No, but it might any minute now . . ."

"Don't you think rain might be something that happens inside of us? If it's raining for lots of people, we see rain. Otherwise it doesn't rain."

"You've been alone for too long. Are those the kind of thoughts you were having when you fainted in the Louvre?"

"I wasn't thinking about anything. My mind was perfectly empty. How many days has it been? Two? Three?"

"Tonight, if you're feeling better, we can go out."

"Where?"

"To La Closerie des Lilas."

"I'll need a cane . . ."

"We'll find one."

"Or maybe a wheelchair . . ."

"We'll see."

"And a blanket over my legs . . ."

"So you're an old lady now?" you say with relief. I can believe anything, if it's said with the proper enthusiasm.

"I'd like . . ."

"Rest awhile. You'll see, things will fall into place."

And to prove your point, you smooth the bedspread over my legs. Then, like those experienced chambermaids who know all the little tricks to make a person feel comfortable, you pull the sheet up to my chin and tuck it in under my shoulders with a pleasant, and very convincing, gesture of being in control.

A Slight, Controlled Unease

"Now! He's alone!"

Vandoros was standing across the room from us, scratching his reddish beard. With his leather gloves and penetrating gaze he looked just like a fox.

"What are you waiting for?" I hissed.

I'm waiting to see where you'll take it. The characters don't convince me, with their gloves and their penetrating gazes. Give me a story. I want to dive in and splash around in the sense of a story. I'd like, as you say. What an idiot: I choose a book by its title.

The waitress brings me my coffee. These days I drink it black. I stopped using milk because I can smell it everywhere: in the sheets, in the fridge, on my clothes. I bend down to pull the white piqué blanket up to her chin and suddenly I'm swimming in a sea of milk.

And to prove your point, you smooth the bedspread over my legs. Then, like those experienced chambermaids who know all the little tricks to make a person feel comfortable, you pull the sheet up to my chin and tuck it in under my shoulders with a pleasant, and very convincing, gesture of being in control.

That's how the story ends. When the first few paragraphs of a story annoy me, I skip straight to the end. When the end annoys me, too, I skip to the next.

"Now turn around. That's it!"

The man gave her a tender slap and lifted her hips back up into the position he preferred. She liked it too, and stretched like a cat before forming a table of flesh with her back.

"Now you're going to feel something hot, then it'll get cold," the man murmured.

"I've had sex before," she answered.

"Not with me."

Got it. A man and a woman in a room. Tables of flesh, crap like that.

"You like to talk while you do it, huh?"

"I like it any old way. Don't move, now, because . . ."

And the heat spread through her, all the way up her back to the roots of her hair. It really was hot. And there was lots of it. Everywhere.

"How long has it been since you've done it?"

"I don't keep track. It's not a performance thing."

"Right, sure," the woman said, sighing into his neck. "Want to try again?"

They make love right there in front of the old men reading their papers, glasses low on their noses. In front of the waitress, who comes over to refill my water. In front of my daughter, who's sleeping in her stroller, now half-opening an eye.

"You awake, honey? You won't even give Mom a chance to find a decent story?"

Ever since she was born I only read short stories. Novels are like murals: it would take a lifetime to finish one. And poetry makes my hormonal issues even worse. I sit there and cry because Hermes, who wanted to be a perfumer, suddenly died at age twenty-seven, in a Syrian seaport. Or because the sky is a blue and gold mistake.

Short stories suit new mothers who love to read. They open the back door for you, let you peek in at reddish beards, chambermaids, women who turn into tables. You sigh into an imaginary neck and it's over.

I wonder how that story ended.

Her body had grown as hard as the tips of her daughter's pointe shoes.

And yet. She had the perfectly reasonable suspicion that she could still fly.

"Nonsense. You can't fly in pointe shoes."

There was a time when my body could balance on its axis and

open so wide in a *relevé* that the breeze would blow into all the pleats of my skirt. Things like that were important to me: the opening, the *relevé*, the breeze. Now I rock the stroller rhythmically, knowing my right shoulder will soon be stiff from the absurd attempt to put to sleep a creature that has just woken up.

"You want me to pick you up? Here, let's see . . ."

Sometimes I read her stories in that lullaby rhythm she likes and get so caught up in the sounds that I lose the thread of what I'm reading. Certain words take on enormous significance—"father," "rain," "aspirin," "pine tree." They break through and say other things. Like the pointe shoes now.

Do you remember how it was, on pointe?

This happens to me often. My thoughts write themselves onto the page, in invisible ink over the printed story.

No, sorry—that thought was mine. I wrote a story about pointe shoes, but I don't have the slightest idea how ballerinas actually feel.

Did I stare into the sun or something? The words flicker out like used lightbulbs.

What I mean to say is, what's missing from my stories is communication, the exchange of ideas. I'm not good enough to know where I'm taking it. And you're not good enough to want to find out.

I pick up my daughter and unscrew the jar of baby food. "Here, how about a little something to eat." With my free hand I flip the book open to a random page.

We have something in common, though. You want to read a story, I want to write one.

"That's it," I whisper. "I've lost my mind." Of course it's now utterly impossible for me to look anywhere but the page.

But isn't this what you were hoping for? For me to speak to you through the lines? And only to you, because you have the gift. Because you're tough, but compassionate. A person with exceptional qualities.

I breathe in milk, I stroke my daughter's back.

Okay, then, let's talk. What do you want to tell me?

"I need literature. I need the consolation it offers. When I was little I would disappear into stories as if they were caves. That doesn't happen anymore. Am I a bad reader, or are you a bad writer?"

Both, probably. Or maybe we just don't suit one another.

"No, I used to understand a lot about you. Little capsules of ulterior motives would burst whenever I'd flip through one of your stories. I saw them, because I had those same ulterior motives."

Apparently.

"So what's wrong with me now? Who am I?"

The waitress shoots me a quizzical glance as she brushes past our table.

"You're trying to tell me we're aging, isn't that it?" I hiss at the page. "You're not interested anymore in being clever or catty. Your skin is losing its elasticity. And you're losing your optimism. The knowledge that you're right. Just like me."

You're wrong, very wrong. We aren't friends.

"Yes, but to me, you're . . . you're my big sister."

I drain the last of my coffee and bang the cup down on the table. A bit of porcelain chips off the bottom.

Don't you mean your little sister? You think I'm incompetent, and I just swallow the insult. But I really don't know, that's why I'm asking: what's it like to walk on pointe?

"Oh, I don't remember. Come on, eat a little more, honey."

She isn't interested in food, only in my book. She wants to touch it, to drool on it, to put it in her mouth and chew on it. Her chubby hands choreograph the empty air. I take a thick cardboard book out of the stroller, suitable for such situations. She starts to pull frantically at a cat's whiskers, a few squashed lengths of reddish-black yarn.

I don't know if you're smart, but you're certainly demanding. You expect solutions from me. What do you want me to do? Write a short story about how to raise kids?

"That wouldn't be bad." I mechanically flip through my daughter's animal book, pointing to anthropomorphic fish with purple scales, elephants with felt ears, dogs with rubber nostrils. "No one cares about things like that. Everyone writes about cars in the rain, couples touching, planets exploding . . ."

"Pointe" is a story about family life. You might like it.

"Is that all you care about? Being liked?"

Don't spit.

"Sorry. I got angry."

You were already angry at the bookstore. You chose a book as if you were choosing a vitamin drink. You want to travel without baggage, without fear. With your baby and your rage.

"I don't want to do anything. Just to watch."

I understand. But I'm a person, too.

"Yes, I know."

Usually you forget. You think I'm made of words.

"If you really must know, I'd prefer to be made of words myself."

You're made of muscles. And they used to be in good shape. Can you tell me what it was like, on pointe?

"My toes hurt a lot. My toenails would get pushed into my flesh. I couldn't forget the pain, not even for a second. I would do an arabesque and instead of thinking about where to throw my weight, I'd be thinking about how much I hurt."

Did you want to be a ballerina?

"What do you think? Isn't that what all little girls want? The pain, the sweat, the shift in your center of gravity, how you rise into the air. It's like childbirth . . ."

The waitress is standing over me, looking down with her big, sad eyes.

"Are you all right? Can I get you something?"

"Could you do me a favor? Could you read a few sentences out loud for me? Here, start there."

"Pointe," she says, and clears her throat. Then, in an expressionless voice, as if she's never read anything before in her life, " '*Now turn around. That's it!' The man gave her a tender slap and lifted her hips back up into the position he preferred. She liked it too, and stretched like a cat before—*"

"Thanks." I pull the book gently from her hand. "I must have imagined it . . ."

"*—before forming . . .*" she continues, before she can stop. "*What does she form?*"

"A table of flesh, with her back."

"Meaning?"

"I have no idea."

She pulls a cloth from under her belt and wipes the dried stains of fruit cream off the table.

“Sometimes books are really boring,” she says.

“And incomprehensible,” I add.

The sun disappearing behind the clouds, the outdoor space heater, the first drops of rain falling on the awning—they all heighten the impression that everything is happening both inside and out. In my heart and in the street. Why else would it start to rain just when I can no longer hold everything in? These parallels make me feel a slight, controlled unease. I fumble in my bag for the red beret.

“Come on, honey, let’s go, before we get caught in the rain.”

A slight, controlled unease.

She could write a story like that.

Pointe

"Now turn around. That's it!"

The man gave her a tender slap and lifted her hips back up into the position he preferred. She liked it too, and stretched like a cat before forming a table of flesh with her back.

"Now you're going to feel something hot, then it'll get cold," the man murmured.

"I've had sex before," she answered.

"Not with me."

"You like to talk while you do it, huh?"

"I like it any old way. Don't move, now, because . . ."

And the heat spread through her, all the way up her back to the roots of her hair. It really was hot. And there was lots of it. Everywhere.

"How long has it been since you've done it?"

"I don't keep track. It's not a performance thing."

"Right, sure," the woman said, sighing into his neck. "Want to try again?"

"How about I smoke a cigarette and you see what you can do for my friend here."

He pointed to an indeterminate spot behind his back, behind the dark mass of the television set.

"So you brought company." She pulled the sheet toward her and meticulously wiped off his sperm. "Let's see who you brought."

"Just take your place, don't worry about the details," the man said, lighting his cigarette. "You're on a roll tonight."

"A roll? I'm on a roll?"

"Now who's talking too much?"

"Must be the bad influences," the woman said. Then she let out a sigh and buried her face in the pillows.

Within seconds, another pair of hands had grabbed her and opened her body wide, until it couldn't open any wider, until her bones creaked.

"That's it!" said the other man in a choked voice.

"No. It's my turn."

She threw him on his back, mounted him, and covered his mouth and nose with her hand, making sure to leave a little opening so he could breathe. She rode her new horse for a while, and when she truly believed she had a horse beneath her, the animal spoke in a human voice:

"I can't take it anymore. I'm going to . . ."

"Say it!"

"I'm going to . . ."

"So say it."

He didn't say it but he did it, and she decided the moment had come to sink into the slippery lake inside of her and let herself get excited by the idea of it. If she thought, "I'm swimming in his sperm," if she thought it very hard and moved in all the right ways, the membranes with the magic rings would open and close and gentle explosions would begin.

"Aren't I better than that cretin?" the man asked, in a disinterested tone of voice.

"You're the best," she said. "The best. Where did your friend go?"

"Him? He must have left. He can't bear the comparison."

"I thought he liked to watch."

"He saw. He saw as much as he could take."

"He should be used to it by now. Do you always pick up women together?"

"It happens sometimes. How about I ask you something?" the man said. And then, in an almost inaudible whisper, in her ear: "Are you married?"

In the dark his eyes looked like puddles of oil, but in the center of each puddle swam something white and thick that she liked. He lit a cigarette, and for an instant she could see his eyes. The fervor in his gaze made her sorry their meeting was so random, so hopeless.

"Why do you care? What does it matter?"

"Some jerk who torments you? That doesn't matter?"

"Oh, he doesn't torment me."

Her eyes were gradually getting used to the dark. She was starting to recognize the masses of furniture, the wardrobe, the armchair with the clothes piled on it any which way.

"So you are married," the man said, smiling sadly.

"I love him. Usually. I don't do this often."

"Love him, or sleep with other men? Because both are related to—"

"What kind of work do you do?" the woman cut him off, wrapping her arms around her knees. The emotion had subsided. She was getting cold.

"I'm in advertising."

"That explains it."

"What do you mean?"

"I'd rather we didn't talk. If I wanted philosophical conversations or marital squabbles, I would've done it with my husband."

The man, who in her imagination would be called "the advertiser," laughed into her hair and whispered in her ear four words that excited her:

"How about another round?"

This time she let him do whatever he wanted. And what he wanted was something incredibly simple. He pushed her down low on his belly and very tenderly, with slow, sad movements that she thought would last forever, gathered her hair from around her face, formed it into a bun at the top of her head and sunk his fingers in like barrettes. Her mind had gotten stuck on the way she'd done her hair earlier. She was thinking about the sudden change in rhythm and mood and how it was changes like this that kept pleasure alive.

"Sorry. I can't," the advertiser said. "You've . . ."

"What?"

"You've sucked me dry."

"I thought that was a good thing," the woman said, sitting up.

She tried to smile, though of course he couldn't see her in the dark. She rubbed her feverish head; thousands of tiny needles had sunk into her scalp while he was pulling her hair. It would be impossible to get them out.

"You've overwhelmed me, I mean. Can you bring me a glass of water?"

She went down to the kitchen, barefoot and naked. Almost immediately the noises wrapped themselves around her: the floor creaked, the fridge quaked, and when she accidentally leaned on the built-in clock on the stove, the kitchen timer shrieked.

"Shut up!" she said to the clock, pounding on it.

She wasn't great with electrical appliances, so she just turned the whole thing off to be done with it. Her head felt as if it were about to burst. Pain had its benefits when she was trying to concentrate on her body and his, but now she just felt uncomfortable.

She groped around in the drawers for a packet of soluble aspirin, tore the wrapper with her teeth, and dropped the tablet into a glass of water. The soles of her feet were stiff with cold. She pulled a white tablecloth from one of the drawers, shook it open, and wrapped it around her shoulders. It was an enormous sacrifice: apart from sex, everything she did was governed by strict rules. The tablecloths were perfectly ironed, the glasses shone, and the silver tray she put his water on was decorated with a crisp linen napkin.

When she went back upstairs, she found the balcony door open, the moon flooding the bedroom with its otherworldly light. The advertiser was gone. She should have seen this coming; when the moment is lost, everything else goes with it. She set the tray down on her dressing table, closed the balcony door, and lay down on the bed. She pulled the comforter all the way up to her ears and fell asleep right away. She held herself back, though, staying on the surface of her dreams so as to control them. When the advertiser appeared and began to ride her, using her hair as reins, she made herself say, "You're hurting me," something not at all suited to a dream. In her erotic dreams she always reacted logically, prosaically. In the bedroom—well, that was a different story.

"Mom, my feet!"

"What's wrong with your feet?"

"They hurt, Mom. I can't take it any more."

"From your pointe shoes? Let me see."

"Not now, I'll be late. The school bus will be here any minute."

She glanced at her daughter out of the corner of her eye and went on buttering her toast.

"We have to do something about this."

"You want me to tell you what we should do?" her husband called from the head of the stairs. "Be patient, that's what."

He was tying his tie. Halfway down the stairs he stopped and looked at them, smiling an enigmatic smile.

"Don't make fun of me, Dad. I'm telling you, my toes are all bloody."

"Yes, but you're the best. It takes sacrifices, haven't we said that before? And you're not going to get fat like your mother."

"Fat?" the woman said. "Who did you call fat?"

She started to throw the toast at him, but he opened his arms wide and gave her a hug. His embrace felt steely and obligatory. When she tried to slip out of it, he slapped her playfully on the behind. He reminded her of the advertiser's friend.

"Did you have a good time yesterday?" he asked her.

"Why, where'd you go yesterday?" their daughter said, her eyes wide.

"I was here, honey. You know how your father likes to tease."

On her way to the bank her jacket got stuck on a branch that was sticking out from some stranger's garden. The branch, weighed down with almond blossoms, had thrust its way through the chain-link fence, refusing to be contained. Her thoughts returned to the advertiser. *Please, let him come back.* She twisted the branch in her hand to free the button on her jacket. The blossoms quivered and fell; only a few remained clinging to the branch. She reached out and shook a nearby branch, too, to see that white rain again. *But he has to come back on his own,* she thought. *I can't invite him.*

Suddenly what she was doing, the shaking of that tree, made her feel like a bully. She looked down at the white and pink blossoms on the sidewalk. So neglected. Cut off from the context that gave them meaning. *What did this tree ever do to me.*

She drank her morning coffee. She poured milk over her daughter's cereal. She got dressed, walked down the street. She pushed her way through the revolving door at the bank. She sat at her window. She counted bills. She said, "Sign here, please." She took her daughter to ballet class. She went back home, changed into something more comfortable. She cooked. She served. She watched television.

The advertiser lived in the middle of her head, behind her eyes, halfway between her ears. There was a place there, a dark little closet, that lit up whenever he reminded her of his presence. And he did that frequently. When she picked out school notebooks with horses on the cover for her daughter. When she stuck her pinky finger into the milk on the stove to test its temperature. When a girl brushed her long hair in some shampoo commercial. *It wouldn't be so awful for us to talk every now and then,* she thought. *If that's what he really needs. We just need to find some other way of talking. Or other things to talk about. Maybe I could tell him about the almond tree. Or my favorite commercials.*

Meanwhile a few other men had come. They had made her into bread, ice cream, an iron. At the crucial moment she always thought of the advertiser.

"So what's going to happen? Are we going to sit here all night?"

"Please, Mom, don't."

They were sitting in the car. She in the driver's seat, her daughter in back.

"I can't make the decision for you. Are you going or not?"

Her daughter stuck her head between the front seats and burst into tears. It upset her to see her daughter like that, so helpless, but was that reason enough to interfere? The best thing to do was to maintain a weighty silence. Maybe shed a few tears. She didn't want her daughter to turn to her, years later, and say it was her fault. She knew from personal experience—children are masters at passing off responsibility.

"The issue is what you want," she said again. "Make two lists in your head. Pros and cons, what you like and what you don't like."

"I like the exercises at the barre. The *pas de chat*," her daughter said through her tears.

"What's that?"

She wiped her eyes.

"When you jump like a cat. And I like taking off my leotard and my tights at the end. And when dad honks the horn when class is over."

"Great. Now what don't you like?"

"I told you, Mom, the pointe shoes. They hurt my toes so much. My toenail is getting pushed into my skin. I can't forget it for a second. I do an arabesque and instead of thinking about where to throw my weight I think about how much I hurt."

"What does your teacher say?"

"The same thing Dad says. Patience and footbaths."

She would have liked to ask her daughter how her toes are supported in the pointe shoes. On the tips? Is there some trick? It's something she had wondered ever since she was a kid. When she would see ballerinas spinning in the air and landing on those pink shoes with the wooden tips and the ribbons twined up their legs, she would wonder if they were happy. How much did it hurt? When they quivered slightly on stage, were they quivering with pain?

She threw her daughter a worried glance in the rearview mirror.

"Maybe you should stop, honey."

"No! I didn't mean I'd stop right away," her daughter said, whirling out of the car like a tornado.

The woman rolled down her window and shouted:

"Be careful!"

Her daughter had already shut the glass door of the dance school behind her, and was disappearing down the hall with that duck-like walk characteristic of young ballerinas.

She braked suddenly on her way into the garage. From the back seat she heard a thump: the pointe shoes falling to the floor. Her daughter had forgotten them, in their pink tulle bag. She stuck them in her purse. As soon as she unlocked the front door, she tripped on the runner in the hall. Her purse, the groceries, her keys, everything fell to the floor.

Maybe I should try putting myself in her position, she thought, fingering the tulle. The two of them wore the same size shoe: the daughter was a giant, the mother a dwarf. First she put on the protective nylon socks, which were stained with dried blood and smelled of girlish sweat. From a distance the pointe shoes looked like huge sugared almonds, but up close they were dirty and very hard at the tips, as if something were living there, something evil and embalmed. She tied the ribbons around her ankles, caressing the silk at each turn. She stood up and walked into the kitchen. *They're like tiny flippers*, she thought. *That's why they all walk like ducks.*

She stood in front of the sink, holding on to the counter, then got up on her toes and let her hands drop for an instant. It was like it had been with the advertiser: brief and painfully insubstantial, something that could assume greater dimensions in her head.

Suddenly she felt sick. She leaned forward, and just managed to make it over the sink in time. When it was over, she rinsed out her mouth and cleaned the sink.

"Come on, give it to me," he said, practically begging.

"No, no." She was speaking more to herself than to the soft shadow moving back and forth above her. She was sweating from the effort. "I can't."

"What's wrong, little girl?"

She sat up, using the sheet to wipe the sweat from her hairline.

"Jesus, aren't you . . ."

"Who?"

"You're the advertiser's friend!"

"Who? Oh, him! You call him the advertiser? I call him—"

"No, don't tell me. Is he here with you?"

"Of course he is. He's an eye-catcher, don't you see him?"

"No, where?"

"Do you like to be watched while you're doing it, or are you trying to insult me?"

"Both, probably."

The man lit a cigarette.

"Great. Just one drag and I'll bring him to you."

"No, now," she said, clutching his wrist.

The man put out his cigarette in the ashtray on the bedside table and turned her face-down in bed.

"You're a bitch," he said, without a trace of anger in his voice.

She waited, feeling her whole body rising to the surface of her skin. She heard the sound of the advertiser's belt. His zipper.

"Aren't you going to say hello?" she asked without turning to look at him. She just arched her back to let him in.

He grabbed her the same way he had before, sinking into her. Furious.

"Aren't you going to say hello?" she asked again. This time her sentence followed the rhythm the advertiser forced on her body.

"I just did."

They clutched one another and rolled around on the bed, tentative, moved.

"What do you want to . . ."

"Whatever you want," the advertiser said.

She rode him first, through the dark, moonless forest of the room. She had her back to his face and whenever she was afraid a branch might stab her in the eye, she leaned her cheek against his knees. She reached the clearing without a scratch.

"Your turn," she said.

"Why are you in such a hurry?"

"I'm not in a hurry. I just missed you."

"When did you have time to miss me?" the advertiser asked disbelievingly.

"Nostalgia has nothing to do with habit. On the contrary, I . . ."

"Hey, aren't you the one who said you didn't want to talk?"

"I don't want you to ask me about my life, my husband. But if you want to talk about us . . ."

"What's there to say about us?"

"What do you advertise?"

"Everything. Cars, milk, tampons . . ."

"No, let's not talk about that. Imagine how it would be if . . . Wouldn't you like for us to go somewhere together?"

"No, I'd like you to turn over and spread your legs."

She wanted to spread her legs, too. Farther than she could. The tone of his voice upset her, reminded her how much she liked to be conscientious and careful. It was his turn to ride. He brushed the horse's mane for hours. Each stroke was, they both knew, just a prelude to the pulling of the reins. Soon the needles sank deep into her skull.

"Mom, Dad, are you sleeping?"

Horse and rider went down.

"What's wrong?" the horse said, tossing its head. The journey from neighing back to human speech was the most difficult part.

"It hurts, it really, really hurts," the girl said.

"Where does it hurt?" she asked, hurriedly pulling her nightgown down. Without her underwear on she was more horse than mother. And the bedroom had a heavy smell, like a stable.

The girl turned on the bedside light.

"What's wrong with you guys?" she asked. "You look funny."

"We were sleeping. You startled us," the man said, slowly pulling the sheet up over his chest. He still seemed like a rider who had fallen from his horse and broken a limb.

"Are you going to tell us what happened?"

"My toes. Look."

The girl lifted her foot and rested it on the bedside table, under the lighted circle of the reading lamp. The skin on her big toe had split open and was oozing pus.

"Jesus!" the two of them said in unison.

"I decided to quit ballet."

"Shouldn't we talk this over in the morning?" the man said.

"No, because in the morning I may have forgotten how much it hurts. I'm telling you, it hurts! I can't stand it anymore!"

"Maybe you could switch out of your pointe class into something else," the woman said.

"It's not the pointe shoes. It's ballet. I get tired. I sweat. When the barre exercises are over, I don't want to do anything. Just to watch."

"Okay," the man said, resigned.

"Why don't we go and put some antiseptic on that?" the woman said.

The girl leaned on her mother's arm as they went out of the room. She was walking like a duck that had been shot.

"Is she asleep?" he asked, taking a final drag.

She nodded.

"What do you say about all this, mother?"

"I feel extremely ridiculous."

The two of them burst into nervous laughter.

"Did you ever imagine it would be like this?"

"What?"

"Just in general."

"Come here."

"Don't even think about it!"

"Why? We were playing so nicely . . ."

"We were playing, that's right."

"And your advertiser? You're just going to leave him like that?"

She turned her back on him.

"I think I'm pregnant."

"What? How did that happen?"

"I said I think, I don't know for sure. Sometimes, with these games, we forget to . . ."

"Did you take a pregnancy test?"

"I'll go and get one. Tomorrow."

"And what will we do if . . ."

Her body had grown as hard as the tips of her daughter's pointe shoes.

And yet. She had the perfectly reasonable suspicion that she could still fly.

Dad and Childhood

"Come here, little one."

I may be little, but I'm not shy. I puff up my chest and mentally prepare to perform another cartwheel.

"Do you want to sit down?" He has fingerprints on his glasses. He's tall and shiny, like the statue of Venizelos in the park.

"No."

I'm supposed to always tell him the truth.

"I thought you might feel more comfortable if we sat down."

There are framed diplomas in his office, and books with leather spines, and drawings done by little kids. There are dollhouses, too.

"Unless you'd rather play," says the man who guesses everything.

He takes notes as I make the dolls do cartwheels on the roof of the dollhouse and triple flips in the air. I push two of them off the roof to see if he'll write that down, too. He does. Then he asks which doll is the daddy, why the mommy is always lying in bed, and why I don't put my sister inside the house. I tell him it's not worth the trouble, my sister is going to die. She just fell off the roof.

"Would you like her to die?" he asks.

"No, but she's going to. Stella told me so."

"Stella? Is there another Stella besides you?"

It's hard to explain. Stella grows up, gets ugly, turns into an old lady, forty years old. She says kids don't stay kids forever. If I tell him that will he yell like Dad did? Everyone's always yelling at me, ever since I told them I saw Stella when she was old.

"Stella is in Dad's movie."

"What's she doing there?"

"She's sitting on the rug with a dog."

"And she talks to you?"

"She says I'm not going to be a gymnast when I grow up."

"Do you want to be a gymnast?"

"Of course."

"Why?"

"Because when you do cartwheels you can see the grass upside-down."

"And Stella says you're not going to make it?"

"That's what she says."

"Do you think maybe you dreamed all that?" he asks calmly. "Sometimes when we're sleeping, our daytime thoughts come back to us, our fears, and . . ."

I'm not listening to what he says. Behind his dirty glasses his eyes are getting bigger. The room is getting smaller. I want to leave.

Finally he calls Dad into the office and tells him to take a seat. Dad perches on the edge of the armchair, barely touching the cushion. The man tells him I'm disconcertingly intelligent.

"What does that mean?" Dad asks.

It means that I'm sensitive and mature. Dad sits back more comfortably, resting his elbows on the arms of the chair. Then the man says we need to encourage my imagination. Dad sits back up on the edge of the cushion.

"Encourage it? More?"

Perhaps they could buy me books, literature, to facilitate the healthy development of my imagination, says the man who guesses everything.

Dad makes a face. "Literature? What kind of treatment is this, anyhow?"

"Treatment for the soul," the man says sharply, as if he doesn't really like Dad. "Books contain encoded solutions, you know."

I've heard that somewhere before.

I've been reading my whole life. It hasn't been an important life, but it's been unique, full of encoded solutions. Somewhere along the line I adopted the manner of that child psychologist. Smudged glasses, eyes like two lakes that drink everything in: poems, essays, novels, short stories. I like short stories best. They're written on a more human scale. Novels seem like desperate attempts at control, and poems like attempts at grandeur. Essays I can write myself, if necessary.

I've met a fair number of writers at literary events. Some of them look at me like I know everything, others like I don't know anything at all. One man once clapped me on the back to show the others we were friends. That's the kind of sincerity you find at those events. I prefer my books and the company of Zacharias.

Basically not much has changed since I was a kid. I live in the same house, behind the park. I keep forgetting the details of my old life as the new one is written over it.

"Come here, Zacharias."

And he comes, with his characteristic eagerness. He flops down on the floor next to me and licks my arm.

"Good boy. Do you want to see Stella when she was little? I was a baby once, too, you know, just like you. Can you believe it?"

The VCR growls.

"Don't worry, it's nothing. We just press the button, see? They turned all the old movies of me into videos. It's what we call the miracle of technology."

I like explaining things to him. How we convert old super eights. Why the iron is hot, why the clothes spin around in the washing machine. Where I go when he stays alone, whimpering, in the house. Why life without siblings has given me a soft spot for dogs, trees, and strange imagery in poems.

"Today is Sunday, silly. Look how hard it's raining. That's why we're just going to sit here and watch the little video I dug out of the storage room. You know, storage rooms are useful places, because that's where . . ."

I could talk to him for hours. He's a perfect listener. His velvety little ears perk right up whenever the tone of my voice changes. And when I've run out of things to say, he lays his snout on my chest.

"So, should we get started?"

I always ask his opinion; it seems only fair. He's my roommate, after all. Sometimes he keeps me from overindulging in alcohol or cigarettes, throwing his head to one side and looking at me like a thoughtful, shrunken little bear. But today he has no attention span whatsoever. He keeps attacking the fringes on the carpet.

"Come on, Zacharias, concentrate. It's starting!"

I press the play button on the remote control and curl up on the rug next to him, hugging my knees to my chest. A black and white girl with bangs appears on the screen, turning cartwheels on a black and white hill. The sun lights up each individual blade of grass separately. The quality of the film isn't very good, but I remember that light. The girl is me. A large bronze man stands behind me, scowling down on my every move.

"That's Venizelos, Zacharias."

Zacharias barks twice at the statue. The little girl with the bangs is happy and sweaty. We see the cartwheel from up close: the perfect arc of her legs, her white tennis shoes, the swish of her bangs in the air.

"Did you see that cartwheel? I could've been a gymnast after all."

I chew on the last walnut from the plate of nuts resting on the arm of the sofa, then lick my finger and dab up the crumbs.

"I was really considering it. A gymnast. Don't you think it would've suited me?"

Zacharias gives a halfhearted growl. The girl in the movie runs down the hill. Her dad is filming everything. Bottle caps. Couples embracing under the trees. The dry grass. The hood of a car.

"Dad wanted to be a director, you know. Back then there were all kinds of legitimate excuses for not achieving your dreams. Poverty, the dictatorship, family obligations . . ."

The dad and the girl are walking toward a gray apartment building behind the park.

"These days we've got money, democracy, and loneliness. What I mean is . . ."

In the film they're unlatching the wrought-iron gate.

"Anyway. That's our hall. Remind you of anything? It would have been a waste of money to redo the whole place. Besides, if you cover the table with books, you can hardly tell it's fake wood."

The girl in the video is overexcited. She's showing off her room to the camera, as if it were a hiding place under the earth, or some useless but entertaining invention.

"Here we see a fine example of a little girl's room, Zacharias. Posters of boys with girlish smiles, stickers, piles of clothes. See that huge pencil sharpener? It was bolted to the table and rumbled like a train . . . And here's the living room."

The girl in the video walks toward us slowly. Her hair is wrapped in a towel and she's wearing pajama bottoms and a faded pink robe.

"Dad, where are you?" she calls.

"On the phone," he answers from the other room.

"The film stopped," the girl murmurs.

"It snapped," I explain.

Outside the window more clouds have gathered. The rain falls from them slowly, as if from dirty, half-squeezed sponges.

"Who are you?" the girl in the movie asks.

"I'm Stella," I say.

The girl's eyes grow wide.

"But I'm Stella," she says, thumping her chest with both palms. "You mean . . . you can see me?"

She takes a step back.

"Can you see me?" she asks.

"Clear as day."

"Well, I have to leave, because . . ."

"Don't be afraid. Look, I remember as if it were yesterday, the film snapped. Now that I'm on the other end it doesn't . . ."

"Doesn't what?"

"It doesn't seem so scary."

"I have to go," she says, out of breath.

"I'm worried about you. Just tell me, are you okay?"

"I'm fine. But Mom . . ."

"I know. And your sister?"

"She's all grown up, she doesn't take me with her anymore."

"Try to love her. She's going to die soon."

"Soon?"

"Yes. She drives too fast."

"Stop scaring me. Who are you?"

"You know who I am."

"No, no way. They'd never get me a dog."

"When kids grow up they can get their own dogs, Stella. No one's going to tell you what to do when you're—"

"Yeah, sure . . ."

"—forty years old."

"Jeez!"

"Tell me about yourself. What do you want to do with your life?"

"With my life?" the girl in the movie asks, as if she'd never thought of it that way.

"Yes, with your life. When you grow up."

"I want to be a gymnast."

"I thought so," says Stella. "Well, you're going to be a book reviewer."

"What's that?"

"A job with books. You'll read lots of books and say which ones you like and why. Cartwheels aren't everything."

"No!" the girl in the movie shouts, putting her hands over her ears.

"I know. But maybe if you can remember a few things . . ."

"Like what?"

"Get out of this house before it's too late. Don't listen to what Dad says about careers and stuff. Don't feel sorry for Mom. And don't take things personally. Awful things are going to happen, but don't take it personally. Everyone gets their fair share of disaster. Oh, and steer clear of a man who's old enough to be your father. Or rather . . ."

"What?"

"Shit. It's useless. Listen, Stella, you'll survive, that's all that matters. There are encoded solutions."

The girl in the movie is crying quietly.

"I know, little one. I wish I could comfort you."

"You're bad," she says. "And you're scaring me."

She takes a few steps backward without looking where she's going, and walks into a little table covered in porcelain figurines, making them clatter and clink. A cat playing with a ball of yarn falls and smashes into a thousand pieces on the floor.

Dad rushes into the living room. He's my age, with the same black bags under his eyes. And most importantly: he's alive.

"Dad, do you see her? Do you see that woman?"

"What woman? Christ, the film snapped! Why didn't you call me, Stella?"

"I did call you. You were on the phone. And then the wall went all white and . . ."

"What's got into you? The film snapped, that's all!"

"I know. And then the woman with the dog appeared on the wall."

"What woman? There's no woman."

"Can't you hear the rain, Dad? It's raining in her house."

He pushes the curtains aside with an air of futile authority. He points to the setting sun, to the grass in the park quivering under the heat, off in the distance behind Venizelos's back.

"Look, Stella! Is everything where it should be? Or are you crazy, like your mother?"

"No, Dad, she's not crazy!" I shout. "I'm not crazy."

The porcelain figurines on the table are breaking inside of me. One after another.

He turns off the projector and darkness suddenly swallows the image.

The living room is gone, and the statue, and the grass.

Dad is gone, and childhood too.

Light

After the rain, the clouds shrank and the sky shone silver. The phone would ring any minute now. I was standing over the receiver when its shrill snarl echoed in the room.

"How are you?"

"Fine. And you?"

"Fine."

"Any news?"

"The same. And you?"

"Same here too."

"Did you think it over?"

"I thought it over."

"Well?"

"I don't know, we'll see."

We hung up and each took a sip of coffee, in her own kitchen, standing in front of her own window, feeling guilty for lying.

She's not fine. I'm not fine.

I began to pace aimlessly back and forth, despite all the chores I still had to finish. Ironing, darning, watering the plants, some rudimentary cooking for one. Cooking for one is a terrible thing. In the end I thought better of it and ate some old bread that had gone soft and smelled like an empty Tupperware container.

The sun peeked out from behind a cloud and came running after me. It nudged its way into the hall, overtook me, and fell hard against the inside of the front door, washing it of its usual dark gray. Then the light got sucked back out through the window, returning to wherever it had come to us from.

Us. I feel like she's always here beside me, seeing what I see. When we were kids, whenever it rained we would burrow under her comforter and talk about how unbelievable it was that one day we would die. To get used to the idea we would bury one another and cry. Then we would hug and sniffle, the rain washing away our thoughts: what had been a bad omen became a source of consolation.

One day she said, "Don't you think rain is something that happens inside of us?"

I didn't understand, but I liked the thought.

"If it's raining for enough people, we see rain," she explained. "Otherwise it's not raining."

Another time she said, "People decide how they're going to die. At a certain point they get tired of living and start to envision their deaths as if they were planning a trip. They say, I'll be wearing my pajamas and walking with an IV pole. Or, I'll be going there with no hair. With black lungs."

"Do you know how you're going to die?"

"I'm going to die in a car accident."

"And me?"

"How should I know? Hold on, wait. You're going to die a slow death. You like to take your time with things. Chemotherapy? I can picture you bald."

She's my big sister. Whatever she says engraves itself in my brain; no rain could ever wash it away. When I first started chemo, I remembered her prediction. She remembered it, too, and suffered a sort of psychosomatic alopecia, so that both of us ended up losing our hair at the same time. That kind of thing happens to us often. One of us will get sick and call the other to tell her about her symptoms, the doctor's appointments, the tests. A few days later, whichever one of us was healthy has fallen ill, too. Years ago my sister developed a kidney stone. Then I got one, too. There was no such thing as laser surgery back then. When they opened us up, they found a stone in each of our right kidneys, as big as a dried-up umbilical cord.

We got married within a year of each other and conceived our children in the same month. Ever since we were teenagers we'd had the same menstrual cycle, so we could be bored together on summer days when we couldn't swim. We liked the same foods, the same movies, the same books. And when each of us necessarily retreated into her own life—husband, kids, work—the telephone took the place of personal presence. We would talk early in the morning and late at night, when no one was around to bother us. My sister no longer said crazy things the way she used to, under the comforter, but every once in a while she would say something that reminded me of her old self. "You're looking out the window right now, aren't you?" she would ask. "Have you ever wondered if what you're looking at might be looking at you, too?" We no longer spoke with the same hunger, and our possible conversation topics had dwindled. These days we were afraid we might get sick if we heard too many unpleasant things all at once. Even when she had the flu and I could hear her sniffling on the other end of the line, she would say she was fine, to protect me. And I did the same for her.

Once our children had left home and our husbands had died, I suggested that we live together. "Better not," she said. That's how it had to be: I had to suggest it, and she had to reject the idea. Every day I would ask her if she'd thought it over, and she would say, "We'll see." Rotten leaves piled up on the windowsill.

My children called every now and then to ask how I was doing. That's a meaningless question when you're old. I'd talk to them about the weather and they'd be impatient to get off the phone. Conversation wasn't useful anymore—it didn't lead to any concrete action.

As the years passed I came to realize that weather is the most important thing in the world, the sole indication of God's presence. That ray from the sun that nudged its way into the hall was trying to tell me something. But I wasn't innocent enough to understand. And if I said anything to my children, they would get worried and hurry over to see me, when all they really needed to do was to look out the window every now and again.

The telephone rang again. I knew who it was.

"I'll come," she said. "But don't make a big fuss. I'll pack a suitcase and come. I only wear two skirts, anyhow, one brown and one black. It's not like I'll turn the whole house upside-down."

"You should rent out your place, so you'll have some money coming in."

"Let's not make a big deal out of it. Let's try it out first, see how it goes."

After we hung up the skies opened again. I did some dusting to show my sister, and myself, that life hadn't gotten the better of me. I even baked a cake to welcome her with. The doorbell rang, she handed me her umbrella, her dripping raincoat, her red beret.

"Stupid weather," she said.

My sister got up every morning and padded into the kitchen in her nightgown. She drank some coffee and ate a few crumbs of bread, like a sparrow. She nodded her head as I talked about the significance of the weather, then got up, leaving her mug in the sink, her crumbs on the table. I brushed them up with a damp cloth, pleased that they swept up so easily from the Formica, together with whatever drops of coffee she had spilled. Then I did the dishes and cooked for the two of us, and since I was dealing with more appropriate amounts, whatever I made usually turned out well. But my sister was always disappointed with my cooking—she always thought there was something missing, not enough salt or sugar or mint. She'd leave the sauce to dry on her plate and go lie down on the sofa.

"Do you think you could water the philodendron on the coffee table?" I asked one day.

She just kept wriggling her hips, searching for a more comfortable position.

"I have an awful headache," she said.

The belt of her robe hung limply from the arm of the sofa.

There was a rotten leaf stuck to the sole of her slipper.

My sister had a whiskey every afternoon, then went out for a short walk or drive. "We have to respect our solitude," she would say. I took advantage of her absence to tidy up a little. I brushed her slipper prints from the sofa cushions, washed the colored-glass tumbler she drank her whiskey from. Then I did some darning, or certain other things I was embarrassed to do when she was there. When she came back she liked to tell me about whatever she had seen on her outing. "Today I walked," she'd begin, or "Today I drove." She would tell me about slippery sidewalks, babies, distracted drivers. Broken streetlights, women walking home from the farmer's market with carts filled to overflowing.

"They push their carts so selflessly. Did I ever do that? I must have, or my children would have starved. But I don't remember anything from that period in my life."

"I do. We're still living in that period."

"You, you're a heroine."

One afternoon I saw her empty tumbler on the coffee table in the living room and got angry. I don't know why I got angry on that particular afternoon. Instead of picking it up, I made a sudden movement and swept the glass off the table onto the floor, where it smashed into a thousand pieces. I'd have liked one of the shards to dig deep into my palm so I could feel the pain, but I carefully picked up the pieces and threw them into the kitchen trash. Then I poured myself a whiskey, too. It burned the roof of my mouth and scratched my throat, going down like broken glass. It went somewhere deep inside me, into some dark, desolate place I didn't like. Did it do that to my sister, too? Did she leave the belt of her robe lying on the sofa because daily life seemed meaningless to her?

It started to rain. The sky knew that I found it unbecoming to cry. It hadn't poured like that since the day my sister moved in. So I thought that if I did exactly what I had done that day, the spell would be broken. I dusted. I baked a cake.

When I finished, it was still raining. Every so often I would look out the window to see if the sky had brightened, but it never had. At one point I saw a red object whirling high in the sky, off in the distance. So small, like a tiny beret.

When my niece called, I knew right away what had happened.

"An accident?"

"I told her a hundred times to get rid of that wreck," she said through her sobs.

"Don't cry, honey."

It was as if I had told her to cry harder. Her voice broke entirely.

"Oh, Aunt, it's just awful . . . They called me in to identify her . . . She was wearing her raincoat and a red beret . . . She looked like a little girl, like a little broken doll . . ."

Would she have thought it self-centered of me if I had compared her pain to mine? After all, I had known my sister for as long as I'd known myself. But my pain wasn't even or smooth. It hitched in places.

"And can you believe, someone robbed her, Aunt! Some passerby pulled her from the wreckage, then stole her wallet right then and there. Can you imagine?"

"People are completely—"

My voice broke, too, but I didn't need to cry. The sky was doing that for me.

"We've come to talk to you about the importance of family. Do you have a few minutes to hear what we have to say?"

The two boys couldn't have been more than eighteen or nineteen years old. They were both wearing suits and ties and something shone on their lapels. I looked closer, and saw little pins with their names engraved on them.

"Are you selling something?"

"No, we're bringing you the message of the Mormon church. We've come to tell you that the Heavenly Father's plan for salvation unites the family not only here on earth, but also in the hereafter."

I stepped aside to let them in and showed them into the kitchen, to the table by the window.

"It's sunny here," I said. "Please, have a seat."

I offered them each a piece of the cake I had made, but they declined. They were right. It was all dried out.

"Thank you for welcoming us into your home. We're representatives of the Church of Jesus Christ of Latter-day Saints."

"Is that some kind of sect?"

"It's a new faith. We're here to tell you about it. But first we want to pray with you. Do you have any objection?"

"My sister died," I said.

"She'll live eternally, in the name of Jesus Christ," the younger of the two boys said, his eyes filling with tears.

"I'm afraid it might have been my fault. I had bad thoughts."

"Let's pray for her," said the older boy.

They bowed their heads, joined hands, and said, "We thank You, Heavenly Father, for guiding us to this home. We ask that You ease this woman's pain and replace it with eternal life, so that she can meet her sister in Your heavenly kingdom. The word of God works through the power of the Holy Spirit, in the name of Jesus Christ. Amen." Then they told me about their founder, Joseph Smith, who went off into the forest one day and had a vision. The prophet Moroni appeared before him and asked him to find the eternal Gospel and translate it in its entirety. It was written on gold plates buried in the ground.

The two boys believed in their prophet. It had been a long time since I'd met anyone who believed in anything with such selfless passion. As they spoke, a hope began to stir in me that my sister and I would meet, and that paradise is a place where it never rains. I read out loud, as they asked me to, from the Book of Mormon, Alma 32: *If ye have faith ye hope for things which are not seen, which are true.*

They made me promise to read a few more verses before going to bed, and to pray. I was very tired and very alone and I said I would. They came again and again, and we prayed together and I said whatever they asked me to say. They were good, honest boys. Whenever I called them to talk about how bad the weather was getting, they always had something comforting to say. And when they came to the house, their upper lips would tremble with emotion. I gave them orangeade and hot chocolate. I also asked them to take my husband's ties, because I couldn't bear to throw them away.

One night I dreamed of my sister. She appeared just as Moroni had, emerging out of a blinding light. She was wearing the long white tunic of a prophet, and the whiteness of that garment was more dazzling than anything I had ever seen in my life. The bedroom lit up as if it were broad daylight, and my sister spoke.

"Are you completely crazy? What on earth are you thinking?"

"Don't be so hard on me. I needed something to believe in."

"Something to believe in? You're in danger of going soft!"

"Did Moroni send you?"

"No, your gullibility did."

"I miss you."

"So pack up your things and come."

"What's it like there?"

"I'm not allowed to tell you what it's like."

"What do I have to do to come?"

"The opposite of what you're doing now. You have to lose all hope."

"But I *have* lost all hope. I don't want to do anything. Just to watch."

"You can't even do that. You can't watch, you can't think. Do you want to live to be a senile old fool? How old are you now? Eighty-five?"

"Eighty-two."

"So what are you waiting for? Come on!"

"Do you think it's my fault?"

"What?"

"Everything. When I broke the glass . . ."

"Who do you think you are, a prophet or something? You don't know anything! You can't even recognize the truth when you see it." As soon as she had passed on her message, all the light in the room gathered around her, swiftly digging a tunnel behind her leading up into the sky. She disappeared into that tunnel of light.

I didn't cross myself when I woke up. I knew she was watching.

I put on my slippers and went into the kitchen. The table was bare and clean, not a crumb in sight. It practically invited you to sit down and make decisions. I boiled some water for chamomile. I poured it into my favorite mug, the one with the almond blossoms on it. I sat down and listened to the rain. How long had it been raining? Ever since the day she died—two whole weeks. I took a swallow and burned my tongue. It felt nice, real, precisely the sort of ordinary thing that happens in life. If I could choose, I'd prefer a slow death, in a hospital, with doctors, intravenous lines, my children gathered at my bedside. I was different from her.

I stirred my chamomile with a spoon.

"You want to have it your way again, huh? You want me to come to where you are. Just like when we were kids, with the comforter. You never budged, I always had to come to your bed. But I'm an old lady now. I can't just die because you want me to. And I could certainly do without all these tunics and tunnels of light."

I crossed myself. But I did it furtively. There was no sense in giving her a reason to laugh at me.

Nail

"I don't like the look of her, that's all," said Mom.

"It's not like we're marrying her," said Dad.

"She's not reliable," said Mom.

"Like I said, we're not marrying her," said Dad.

Then they fell silent. I stared at the house through the space between the front seats, at the downward slope of the hill, the asphalt unwinding like a dirty ribbon.

"Basically it's a ruin," said Dad.

"You know I like ruins," said Mom.

"Get over it," said Dad.

"Get over shit," whispered my sister, who had been dozing with her head resting on my shoulder. I dissolved into giggles.

"Can't you two keep quiet for one minute?" said Mom.

She turned in her seat to glare at us. There were two wrinkles between her eyebrows. Two slitted, squinting eyes.

"What did the kids do to you?" said Dad.

"They didn't do anything. It's the heat, and her unreliability."

"Let's go and stand in the shade, then."

"Fine, everyone out. We're going into the church."

The church was small, but it dominated the hilltop, sitting up above the house. Inside, it was damp and dark and smelled of mildew. Mom lit a candle. Light licked the walls, and we saw a woman watching us with sad, yellow eyes.

"Which saint is that?" Mom asked.

The saint, whoever she was, was showing us the nail-marks on her hands and feet. They were ringed with dark-red dried blood.

"I thought only Christ got crucified," said my sister.

"It could happen to anyone," said Mom.

"Anyone?" Dad asked.

"Do me the favor," said Mom.

The salt from our afternoon swim had dried on our backs while we were waiting for the real estate agent. I sat down on the cement step in front of the altar and drank some water from my plastic bottle. It was warm and smelled faintly of sausage.

Dad went over and lit a cigarette with Mom's candle.

"Are you crazy? You're going to smoke in here?"

Dad gave her a sharp look and took a deep drag on his cigarette.

"What you're doing is . . . it's . . ."

"I'll do as I please, I was born here. I've walked these hills, been scratched by their thorns."

"I'm not telling you where to get scratched, I'm telling you where not to smoke. What kind of example are you setting for your children? Is that how to teach them respect?"

Dad ground out his cigarette with his shoe as if he were trying to annihilate it. Then he went out into the courtyard.

"Is it all right with you if I smoke under this tree? Or is that sacrilege too?"

The tree stood all alone beside the church. Mom and I sat down on its roots, which formed a tangled pile of motionless snakes. The trunk had been whitewashed at some point, but the white was flaking off, like the polish on my sister's nails.

"Someone needs to invent a telephone for these kinds of situations," Mom said.

Dad lit another cigarette. By the side of the road, the dried weeds were quivering in the heat rising from the hood of our car. You could have fried fish on it. Not that any of us was hungry. We'd ordered the whole menu at the taverna.

"I say we should leave," my sister said. She had come out of the church, too. She was playing with a little yellow candle, uncoiling the wax from the wick. "Mom, can't you see it's a wreck?"

"Your eyes are the wrecks," said Mom. "Old houses are alive, full of history."

"This particular one seems to have breathed its last," said Dad, and my sister giggled. I didn't. Mom always feels alone in these situations. Someone has to take her side. And that someone is me.

"What do you say, Stella? Shall we go and take a look around?" Mom said without looking at the other two.

"Sure," I said.

"Watch out for falling beams," my sister said, casting a conspiratorial glance at Dad, as if they were the parents, and Mom and I the kids.

The moment we stepped out of the shade we were bathed in sunlight. Our flip-flops slipped on the downward slope, making a funny sound, like someone chewing gum. The crickets were shrieking. Mom took off her shirt, so that her only top was her bikini top with the almond blossoms on it. I did the same.

"Maybe we'll get a tan," I said.

Mom smiled and held out her hand. The air around her smelled, as always, of Nivea lotion. But as soon as she opened the decaying front door of the house, the air, far and near, suddenly smelled like a rotten egg.

"This way. Don't be afraid," Mom said.

We walked through the dark to the far end of the room. Mom felt around, found a window, and unbolted the shutters. Sunlight sliced through the house, right to the heart.

"Oh my God!" said Mom, resting one palm on the string in the middle of her bikini top. With her other hand she pointed to some faded paintings on the ceiling. Grapes and other kinds of fruit.

"Mom, look! There's a fireplace!" I knew how much she liked fireplaces. Each weekend we drove all over the hills and shores of Attica looking for a vacation home, and by now I had learned where her soft spots lay.

Mom touched the marble lion's paw on one side of the fireplace without the slightest sign of disgust.

"Can you imagine how beautiful it could be? This would be the living room. And over there, the dining room . . ."

I squinted my eyes and could picture it right away. By now I knew exactly what she wanted, where the sofa would go, and the rest of the furniture we didn't have room for in our other house. Bit by bit this house would start to replace that one, because it was better for us to live like this, in the country, waking up with the cock's crow, drinking milk straight from the goats. Life would be beautiful and simple. Mom could paint her targets just like she always wanted to. Only here we wouldn't call them targets, even if they were still the same black and white circles. And we wouldn't play darts with her canvases, or make Mom cry because we had no respect for anything. Our fresh start would erase all the bad moments; we would share responsibilities, like a proper family. And if things got tough Mom would have the church close by. She could sneak off to light a candle and cry.

Once I had put all the furniture in its proper place, I started to get bored. So I pretended we were archaeologist-explorers and the fireplace was the entrance to a secret hiding place. I touched the other lion's paw. Nothing happened.

Mom was looking at the irregularly spaced beams over our heads. Sunlit motes of dust were falling and dancing between them.

"You think there's something up there? Skylights?"

"Where?"

"Up there," Mom said. "Where else would the light be coming from?"

"So we'll sleep in the attic?" I started jumping up and down with excitement.

"If there's an attic, we'll move right away, how's that?"

"Mom, we have to fix it up first! How could we live in this place? It's a wreck!"

"True," Mom said, and turned her back to me.

I'd spoiled it for her. The sunlit dust was falling more sparsely from the beams. I had to do something to make it thicker again.

"Look, Mom! A ladder!" There was a crude ladder propped up against the wall, half hidden in the dark.

"Okay. You stay here. I'm going up to take a look at our bedrooms."

The rungs creaked as she climbed. The creaking tightened some spring inside me.

"Be careful!" I said.

Outside the house a tinkling female laugh pealed over the hum of the crickets. The real estate agent must have come.

"Stella, you can't even imagine . . ." Mom called down. "There are no walls up here, no nothing, just beams. If we fix the roof and put new frames in the skylights, we can lie in bed watching the rain fall."

Mom and I lying in bed, sharing secrets. Mom's fingers covered with dried paint, a knitted afghan over our legs, rain drumming against a glass pane over our heads. We have to be careful getting out of bed so we don't hit our heads on the ceiling. The skylight brings us closer to the sky. The secrets we share are dark and beautiful. They have the power to lift us up.

The dust started dancing again.

Suddenly there was a loud creaking sound and the dust flew in from all sides, bright and all-powerful, and pulled my mother down with it. Her body fell amidst planks and nails, but when it hit the floor I didn't look. I hid my face in my hands and cried out her name until my throat was dry.

Dad and my sister came running into the house with the real estate agent, and Mom said, very faintly, "I'm alive."

My breath had caught in my throat. I breathed in those words. I turned around and looked at her. She was trapped under some planks and a huge nail had pierced her calf and come back out near the ankle, right by the bone.

Dad shouldn't have smoked in the church. My sister shouldn't have told us to watch out for falling beams.

And I shouldn't have been such a coward. I should have put my arms out when she fell. I should have done whatever I could to save her.

"I can't feel anything. Anything at all," Mom said.

"Don't talk," Dad said, and began to stroke her hair.

The dust that had gathered in her hair started to dance. I looked again at the nail. It was pointy and would leave a big mark, just like in the icon. Luckily, Mom was wearing her bikini top with the almond blossoms. And her eyes weren't yellow.

What Will You Do Next?

The office smelled of burnt wire. The remains of my morning coffee were drying on the bottom of the cup. A silly notion came over me. Perhaps it happens to others, too, I couldn't say. The loneliness, the boredom, the piles of papers by students who didn't even know who Demosthenes Voutiras was. I picked up the phone and called my house, though I knew the kids were in school and my wife at her office. I just wanted to hear my voice on the answering machine and hang up. A little joke.

"Hello?" the voice said.

It was my voice, sounding as if it had just woken up.

"Who is that?"

"Who are you looking for?" the voice asked.

I hung up and called right back.

"Hello?" the voice said.

"Who is that?"

"Who are you looking for?" the voice asked again.

"Enough already. Who are you, and what are you doing there?"

"What am I doing in my own house?" asked the voice.

It was my voice, only it wasn't coming from my mouth.

"I'm going to hang up and call again," I said, more to myself than anything else, then quickly slammed down the receiver before the voice had a chance to respond. I uncapped the whiskey I keep for difficult moments and took a swig straight from the bottle. The alcohol skewered my stomach. I dialed my home number again.

"Hello?" said the voice.

"There's no reason for us to argue," I said. "Just tell me who you are. And what you want."

He said he was the owner of the house and the telephone line.

"Well, if you're the owner, as you say, what are you doing there at this hour? Don't you have a job?" I asked.

He told me that he usually sleeps until afternoon and works at night.

"What kind of work?" I asked.

"I'm a writer," my voice answered.

At that point I started to laugh.

"I don't understand. What's the problem?" my voice said.

"The problem, for starters, is that you don't exist."

"No, you don't exist." The voice had the same patient tone I use when I'm talking to the children, or to the guy with a screw loose who lives in the basement apartment of our building.

"No, you don't exist, and whenever you try to grab hold of something, it seems such a . . ."

"Such a . . . ?"

"Such a preposterous exercise."

"What do you mean? For as long as I can remember I've wanted to be a writer," my voice said.

"Yeah? And what masterpiece did you write?"

He told me he'd only written one book, about hypothetical encounters with himself in various places and situations. When he really wanted to stay in some particular place but ended up leaving, he would imagine how it might have been if he had stayed. He left his aura there, in a way—that's what he said. For the purposes of the book he had learned to split himself down the middle, to do what he wanted to do and what he ought to do at the same time. "It's an important skill," he said, "especially when you're faced with tragedy. You can't change reality, but you can split yourself into two."

"Split yourself into two?"

"Yes. You can hit the road, but also freeze right where you are, full of remorse."

Madness, I thought.

"And what work do you do?" he asked.

I told him I taught modern Greek literature at the university.

"Oh, of course. Now I know who you are."

I uncapped the whiskey again. I loosened my tie and slipped my free hand into my armpit, under my shirt. I wanted to touch something that was mine.

"Just cut the crap," I said.

"Are you sitting down?" my voice said. "You should probably sit down. You're not going to like what I have to say."

"Don't tell me . . ."

"Seriously. You're really not going to like it."

"Say it, I can take it."

"You called me because you're experiencing an acute existential crisis. And you're experiencing an acute existential crisis because you're a complete fabrication."

"Of course," I said. It didn't come out quite as ironically as I had intended, so I said it again. "Of course, that explains it."

"I'm sorry," my voice said. '"I'd have liked to give you life, something to believe in, but . . . I had a good idea, and that was that. I've never really been able to finish anything."

"Anything," I repeated like an echo.

"You can mock me as much as you like. And you can hope. You have every right to imagine a life for yourself and to proceed within it, as far as you can."

"Are you serious? Thanks for that unexpected generosity."

"I don't want to push the issue, but . . . what will you do next?"

"Next when?"

"When you leave the office," my voice said.

"I'll go home. And I suggest you make yourself scarce by the time I get there," I said.

"You won't be coming here," my voice said. "There is no other 'here' for you."

"If you mean the only place I really feel comfortable is my office, you've hit the nail on the head."

"No, I mean that the office is your finite universe," my voice said. "That's where you exist. I don't know where else to put you or what to do with you. Others call me sometimes, too. Every so often they start to feel alive, just like you. They usually figure they've been working too hard, or are plagued by unfulfilled dreams, or think they're starting to lose their minds, but really it's all my fault. It's all me."

"Can I give you a friendly suggestion? Find yourself a good doctor. There's a name for what you've got: megalomania."

"You think I'm playing God, huh?"

"I'm going to hang up now."

I was tired of the conversation. And there was no more whiskey.

"Wait. You're a lecturer in modern Greek literature, right? You write book reviews for a newspaper. Whenever you finish a really good book, your right hand shakes. And whenever the going gets tough, you drink. You have an entirely ornamental family. Two kids. And a lover who adores you, even though you treat her like shit. You like to pull her hair in bed. How do you think I know all that?"

"A+ for research," I said.

"The question is, how are you going to break away from what I've written and do what you want to do? Desire and obligation, see? I gave you a pretty superficial role. I was never very good at creating characters. It only worked once, by chance."

"Take my advice. Find a good psychiatrist."

"I have a good psychiatrist," my voice said. "But he can't help."

"Is your situation that dire?" I said.

"You have every right to be angry. You sit there all day like a cucumber. You're bored out of your mind, correcting papers. I know, it's tough."

"Yeah, fine. I'm hanging up now, you crazy fool."

"Wait a minute. If you find your way here, it'll mean you're more real than I imagined, right?"

"I'll find my way, all right. The question is, where will you hide?"

I slammed down the receiver. I tore open a packet of soluble aspirin with my teeth. As it was dissolving in a glass of water, I gathered up my glasses, keys, and wallet, and tossed them into my briefcase. My grading could wait. I needed to finish with this first.

I put an arm in one sleeve of my raincoat. The other sleeve dragged behind. I groped for it blindly.

I must have drunk more than I thought, because I couldn't find the door.

The Most Wonderful Moment

"Could I get one of those?"

He pushes his cigarette case in my direction. The second hand on his watch screams, leave, leave, leave.

"Thanks."

"Do you need a light, too?"

"If it's not too much trouble . . ."

He leans over slowly. Apparently his stomach is getting in the way. His lighter slips from his hands and drops silently onto the rug.

I bend down and grope for it blindly. "Don't worry, I've got it."

The lighter is hot. It must have been warmed by his hand.

He sinks back into the cushions of the sofa and sighs.

"I hope you at least have lungs to smoke it with?"

His irony. You have to endure it, even encourage it, if you want him to pay you the slightest bit of attention.

"What's wrong? Are you crying?"

"No, the smoke just got in my eye."

The more I rub it, the more it waters.

"And I suppose you don't have any tissues in your purse. Young ladies today don't seem to carry tissues anymore."

"Do you believe the world used to be a better place? Back when young ladies carried lace handkerchiefs with them wherever they went?"

"What a wonderful technique! You wait for your interlocutor to say something, then push his thought to its extreme. Then you call yourself a reporter, and our conversation an interview."

I don't know where to look. It's a small room, just the Oriental rug with the almond branches, the coffee table, the sofa, and us. And a handful of books on a shelf against the wall: Vizyinos, Foucault, Guy de Maupassant. All men, and all insane. He must give away, or throw away, all the books he receives from young admirers, crackpot writers, and publishers hoping to put out his collected work someday. The only thing he said that I managed to jot down: "Harmless people write dangerous books. You flip one open to a random page and feel like killing the harmless person who wrote it, so he'll stop fouling up the place. Printing is pollution. A wound."

Then everything went horribly wrong. I suggested that mediocrity was just as necessary as genius, and he started to cough so hard and so relentlessly that I was afraid something might break loose from the back of his throat. I asked if he wanted me to bring him a glass of water. Only the thirsty drink water, he said, and he was either sated or tired—*koresmenos* or *kouresmenos*, I wasn't sure which.

"You're tired?" I asked, because it seemed like the milder option.

He stood up and walked—or rather rolled, he's so short and round—over to the bookshelf, pulled down the big Dimitrakos dictionary, and pinned his gaze on me.

"Koresmenos," he read in his booming voice. "Glutted, satiated; cloyed or surfeited by indulgence of appetite. And the verb: *korennimi, koreso, ekoresa*. Oh, and here's another word you should learn. *Korevma*. Virginity."

Then trouble started to fall like rain. The room was so stuffy, so full of mounting anxiety, that I yawned; he thought I was bored. I asked him if he was writing anything at present; he said I was being indiscreet. I asked for a cigarette, and we ended up talking about thoughts being pushed to their extreme.

Ever since I was a kid I had dreamed of meeting him. I read his stories stretched out on the couch, the one with the checked wool and the big buttons, and when I dozed off I would dream of crying fish or pine trees that grew upside-down. His books, lying open on my chest, made my heart beat faster. His author's bio at the end of each volume would play like a movie in my head, with me starring in all the roles. I was the young writer who took a job at a newspaper to support his family after his father was killed during the Occupation. I was the dead father, and the domineering mother who got left behind. I was his first wife, whose wealth allowed him to concentrate on his writing. And his second wife, the one who made him hate women. I was his first male lover. His editor. I was even the Great Writer himself.

My desire to imitate him led me to the newspaper where I work today. Through my job, I too would find men and women to love or hate with a passion, and afterward I would pick them apart for the sake of whatever story I was writing. And though my conscientiousness, my endless hours of work, and my specialization in literature had all prepared the ground for a meeting between us, I kept resisting. How many years passed that way? Ten?

What it took, in the end, was for the arts editor to assign me an interview with him. I put it off, and a week later she reminded me, and said it was pressing. My voice shook on the phone when I called to make the appointment. By then I had done thousands of interviews with poets, novelists, essayists, translators. I'd entered hundreds of homes whose owners had endless shelves of books and believed in words more than anything else in the world. I'd found dozens of ways to introduce a particular topic, to talk around it, or even to forget it altogether. Everyone at the newspaper said my interviews had a certain "something": the almost pathological curiosity of a creature from some other planet trying to understand the habits of human beings. I had recently been given a promotion. They kept assigning me more and more interviews—not just with writers, but with politicians, athletes, economists. And I always did an excellent job. In fact, there were people who bought the paper solely for the interviews I did. I don't know what it was that made people open up to me. They would tell me the kinds of things people usually only think about after a funeral, when the mind clears out all but the most elemental of thoughts.

"*Korevma*," he repeats, staring at me with a challenge in his eye. "Let's see. Remember what it means?"

"You really think there's something virginal about me?"

Passive-aggression. It helped me once, with a self-destructive ship owner.

"Everything about you is virginal. You try desperately to mold it into something that can pass for experience, but you're not fooling me, my dear."

"'My dear'? That's the phrase you used to use to avoid giving your characters names. Everyone called one another my dear. And they all fought like cats, tearing at one another's fur, just like us."

"Is that why there isn't a hair left on my head?" he asks, rubbing his bald scalp. "Nor on yours, I see . . ."

"It's from the chemo."

Aggressive self-pity, my ultimate weapon.

"Ah. And now you expect me to beg for your forgiveness?"

No, I expect him to heal me, just as he healed the characters in "The Hale and the Hearty," a short story in which he devised a kind of magical psychotherapy: the sick shake off their psychosomatic symptoms by returning to the moment when they uttered their first excuse.

"I'm fine." I try to laugh, but it comes out as a snort. "These days I'm as hale and hearty as they come."

"You've done your homework, I see. How long did it take you to skim through my books? A weekend? Or am I overestimating?"

A lifetime. A lifetime of veneration, a weekend for the deposition from the cross.

I shrug. "What does it matter to you?"

"It doesn't. Just making conversation. Will you excuse me for a minute?"

He shuts himself in the bathroom. Time for me to stretch my legs and conduct a little random-sample research. I pick three books off the shelf and open them to see if he takes notes in the margins, or underlines passages—a few tricks I've thought up for the most difficult cases. Nothing. His books are immaculate, the bindings unbroken. The only aesthetic touch on his desk is a blue porcelain cat playing with a ball of yarn, sitting atop the telephone and electric bills. Trivial sums. He obviously doesn't talk much on the phone, or cook, or keep too many lights burning.

I hear a thud. Something shudders, heaves, then shudders again.

"Are you all right?"

I go over to the bathroom door and listen carefully. Not a sound. The room looks larger and more welcoming from a distance, and without us in it. There are just a few steps between me and the end of the hall, where the bedroom must be. I gently push open the door and see something that looks like an enormous elephant's ear. It's the bottom half of his bed, impeccably made up with a plain gray bedspread. The color of the blanket and the absence of a single discernable wrinkle remind me of his stories. But that kind of austerity doesn't suit me anymore: it betrays the fear of making a mistake, not the fear of excess, as I once thought.

I hear a moan.

"Are you all right? Do you need something?"

The moan gives way to a rustling, dragging sound.

"I slipped," he whimpers.

"What should I do?"

"You can open the goddamn door!"

I push as hard as I can, but his weight is pressing on the door from the other side. I kick it. I pound on it a few times with my elbows. Then with my fists. I take a running start and push with all my weight. The wood responds with hollow thuds. To boost my courage I think back to the absolute worst moments of our conversation in the living room. I pretend that I'm hitting the Great Writer himself.

"For God's sake, I locked the door," he says.

"Can you reach up and unlock it?"

"If I could, would I be in this ridiculous situation right now?"

"Did you break anything?"

"I don't know," he gasps.

I'd like to tell him that his bones are very well protected by all the layers of fat on his body, but that's the kind of thing he would think up. There's no reason for me to struggle with his thoughts anymore.

"Perhaps it would be better if I called for help?"

"No, I just need to lift up my hips. Then I'll raise my hand, and . . ."

"One thing at a time. Let's start with your hips. Are you on your back? Can you prop yourself up on your elbows?"

"I have no idea what position my body is in. All I know is that my watch is right next to my ear and the ticking is driving me crazy."

His watch that was saying, leave, leave, leave—now it's saying, come.

"Imagine yourself in some particular position. Then move according to that position."

He heaves a heavy sigh.

"I imagined the wrong position."

"Imagine another."

The key rattles and the Great Writer howls.

"What happened?"

"I pulled it out of the keyhole! What an idiot! I couldn't turn it, I would have torn something."

"Can you push the key under the door?"

First I see the teeth, then the flat part with the rather useless hole in the middle. I turn the key in the lock. His shoe is blocking the door. I move his foot aside to clear a space, then go in the only way I can: pushing.

He's lying face down on the tile floor, in a very private position. His belt is loose, his pants down around his thighs. Fortunately his underwear is white, so I can pretend it's just a natural continuation of the white of his shirt. I avoid looking at the stretches of exposed skin: I'm ashamed they exist, ashamed that the Great Writer has a body like the rest of us.

I turn him over onto his back and drag him by his shoes toward the bedroom. The friction makes his shirt ride up even higher. His little shriveled penis sways gently this way and that. I feel sorry for it all, for my bad thoughts, his bad thoughts—one look at that poor, defenseless thing is enough, dear Lord. Then, because the Lord isn't doing anything, I reach out and pull down his shirt from both sides, as if it were a theater curtain.

"Thank you," he says. His eyes are deep and wet. "Thank you, my child."

And just like that, I become a child again. I think about my life from the beginning, in a natural, elemental way.

"I wanted it more than anything else in the world," I say, slurping my whiskey.

"And what happened?" he asked, slurping his, too, but with little sips.

"Life, you know . . ."

"No, I don't know."

He doesn't like to feel indebted. I spoiled his self-sufficiency, and now he's spoiling mine.

"Okay, not life. My big sister."

"What did she do?" the Great Writer says with a roaring laugh. "Did she forbid you to write?"

"Something like that."

Outside the bedroom window, behind the clouds, enormous peaches lie rotting.

"How can anyone do that? And if they can, why don't you write about that, too?"

"Yeah, sure, literature of defeat . . ."

"Better that than the defeat of literature."

By the time I step into the elevator he'll have forgotten about me. I'll be just another example of wasted effort, nothing more.

"I turned seventy two weeks ago," he says. He smoothes the gray blanket over his legs, sketching his thoughts in circles in his lap. "Every day I wake up and wonder what's the sense of it all. In my weaker moments I think there's something playing with us. In better moments I think we're playing with that something. You know, like a cat chasing a ball of yarn, believing the yarn is alive, though really the cat is the one making it move."

No, I don't know. And I'm no longer paying attention to the details that might help me recreate the atmosphere later on. I'll say he refused to give the interview. He wouldn't even open the door.

"You're young," he continues. "You just open a door and push those thoughts into some dark corner. But at a certain point the thoughts start to come back on their own. You open the oven, thoughts. You open a letter, thoughts. You lift the lid of the toilet, and what do you see . . ."

A wave of nervous laughter breaks over him. His laughter pulls me in, too, and we laugh together, the Great Writer slapping his open palms on the bedspread, me pounding my feet on the floor.

"Oh, yes, the lid of the toilet . . ."

"How old are you?" he suddenly asks.

"Thirty."

"Do you know how wonderful it is?"

"What do you mean?"

"That age," he sighs. "It's the most wonderful moment."

Night has fallen. We should really turn on a light. The Great Writer's silhouette stirs in the bed.

"Come here. I have an idea. How about we hold one another for a while? For God's sake, don't get the wrong idea! Surely you know that I . . . Of course you know. All the details of my life have become grist for the gossip mill."

"What exactly are you asking me for?"

"A hug, a human embrace. No one hugs old people. So you tell yourself you don't really need it, you can live without it—and besides, how much longer can you possibly live?"

"Please, don't say things like that."

"Come here. I'll take something from you. You'll take something from me."

"How, by osmosis?"

"Why not?"

I drain my whiskey and climb up onto his high bed. I let his hand fumble around on my back.

"Amazing," he whispers. "You have a back."

His neck smells of whiskey and freshly toasted bread. He squeezes me tight for a few endless seconds. I hug him back, as hard as I can, because I know I'm an independent being, and soon I'll peel away from him again. Then he pats me a few times on my shoulder-blade.

"Well, that was . . ." He's searching for words.

"What?"

“That was the kind of thing that only happens in stories.”
“Yes, but it happened to us.”
“It happened to us? Do you really believe it happened to us?”
The darkness around us has thickened.
I don’t know what he expects me to say.

The Firefly Hunt

"I'd like to see them every once in a while."

"You'd like to see them?" she asked, spitting the words out one by one.

"Yes, if you don't object."

He imagined her sitting disheveled in her chair, a wreck in a purple robe.

"You'd like to see them? Have you lost your mind?"

"Fine. It was just a suggestion."

The conversation was taking place over the phone. She couldn't see him scratching his chin or pulling at his earlobe. She had no way of knowing that he was a wreck, too, and utterly at her mercy.

"With you everything always starts with a suggestion. Then the suggestion becomes an idea, and the idea becomes reality," she said, gripping the arm of her chair.

"Just call it a professional perversion."

"Except those perfect families skipping happily through fields of wildflowers only exist in your stupid commercials, dammit, only in—"

She stopped in mid-sentence to catch her breath. When she was younger she could scream. Now, fuses blew in her brain, one after another.

"Please, calm down."

"I pity you, you poor thing."

"Why? Because I want to see them? What's so pitiful about that?"

His ear had gone red from his pulling it. He was pinching himself, hurting himself, in an effort to make himself look like her.

"Talk it over with them," she finally said.

"They'll eat me alive if you don't talk to them first."

"That's your problem. I have other things on my mind."

She had nothing at all on her mind, she just liked to assert her detachment from things. It had become her role after the accident, to retreat into herself and sit brooding like a hen on an empty void.

"Okay, I get it, you don't want to help."

"To help? To help?" The words clattered like metal spoons falling in a heap on the floor.

"Fine, forget it. Just pretend I never said it."

But she had already hung up.

He went into the bathroom to look at his ear in the mirror. It was swollen from his picking at it. He took a little of the cream She had bought for him and spread it on in circles, the way She had shown him. She looked after him. And since he had spent the past several years nursing someone else, these days he enjoyed getting sick, being taken care of, feeling unimportant.

"You're unimportant," she had told him as they were sitting in their lawyer's waiting room. She had spoken without her usual contempt. Calmly and tiredly, as if she were saying, The weather's changed, or, I'm bored. Sometimes, in the car, as he's waiting at a light with the rain pounding against the windshield, he hears that phrase in his head, spoken in her voice. The rain takes it up and repeats it, with the windshield wipers keeping the rhythm: Unimportant, fcht, unimportant, fcht, unimportant, fcht. The radio broadcasts incomprehensible words.

"I told her I want to see them every once in a while."

"Oh," She said, biting her bottom lip. "And?"

"She says I should talk it over with them."

"And?"

He chewed several times before answering.

"I don't know how," he said.

They were eating at a badly-ventilated taverna in their neighborhood. They knew that their clothes would stink afterward, but they liked the food. The entrails, the meatballs, the fried zucchini. It seemed like a miracle, the fact that they were living together now and didn't have to eat souvlaki in the car, didn't have to find excuses to slip out of a room long enough for a phone call.

"Why don't you go and find them?"

"I don't know."

"You could wait outside the school. Take them for a drive. Or for pizza."

He'd tried. Sometimes he would follow them in the car. A battalion of boys and girls would troop down the hill, their ranks growing thicker as he got closer to the school, but his girls stood out even from a distance. They were tall, like him, and walked side by side, always in black. The older of his two daughters would be gesturing, the younger nodding her head. For years he thought he loved Christina more—she was the offspring of absolute desire—but the way Stella bowed her head reminded him of himself, how trapped he'd felt. On one of those afternoons he'd had the impression that Stella had sensed his presence. She had antennae, like him.

"I'm no good at those things," he said.

"What things?"

He flattened the remains of a meatball with his fork.

"At giving explanations."

She caressed him between his fingers.

"You don't need to give explanations. Just a look is enough."

He released the emergency brake and let the car roll along beside them, until they saw him and stopped.

"You . . ." said Stella.

"What are you doing here?" said Christina.

He'd gotten used to their backs, but it had been a long time since he'd seen their faces. Their features had grown hard. His older daughter had emerged abruptly out of puberty, and her eyes emitted an otherworldly light. His younger daughter had two large, purple pimples on her neck, right at the neckline of her black sweater. He didn’t understand why two girls, aged fourteen and seventeen, would be dressed in black. Even their umbrellas were black.

“I missed you guys,” he said, and blinked several times, until his eyes finally dried.

The girls stood there in silence. They were waiting for something.

“I wanted to tell you . . . I tried for so long . . . I’m so sorry, about everything.”

“If you were sorry you wouldn’t have done it,” Christina said. Her eyes narrowed, giving off that light again.

“When you’re older, you’ll understand that it has nothing to do with you.”

“It has to do with Mom,” Stella said, looking down at the sidewalk. ‘“And Mom has to do with us.”

Then, as if they had agreed upon it ahead of time, the girls started walking again.

“Can I take you for ice cream?”

“Are you crazy? Can’t you see it’s raining?” Christina said.

“Fine, then. An orangeade.”

Suddenly it occurred to him that this was exactly how teenage boys would approach them, by letting off the emergency brake, turning toward the open passenger’s side window, and asking them out for an orangeade.

“We’re not kids anymore. We don’t drink orangeade,” Christina said.

“And even if we do, Dad, we’re still not kids.”

Stella had called him Dad.

“So what do you drink these days?”

“Whiskey,” said Christina.

“Fine, then. Let’s go for a whiskey.”

He couldn’t believe his ears.

It was the middle of the afternoon but the sky outside the Galaxy Bar was already dark. The girls shook out their umbrellas and perched on stools at the bar. That meant they wouldn't have to face one another, which was good. He ordered a whiskey for Christina and two orangeades, for himself and Stella.

"They'll think I'm a dirty old man," he said, watching his older daughter down her whiskey.

"Aren't you?" Christina said, shaking her glass until the ice cubes rattled. "How old is She, anyhow? Twenty?"

"Twenty-five," he answered, then asked the barman to add a splash of vodka to his orangeade.

"Same difference," Christina said, draining her drink. "Can I have another?"

He felt like laughing and crying at the same time. His daughter was already tipsy and the conversation hadn't even begun.

At some point, of course, it did. The whole time they talked, Stella sucked at her orangeade through a straw. Whenever they disagreed about something or described contradictory memories, her canines sank into the purple plastic.

After he dropped them off he realized that he hadn't touched his ear a single time. And even now he was soothed by the scent the girls had left behind, of cinnamon and sour lemon. They had kissed him on the cheek as they left; they'd come to love him again in just a few hours. Of course in Christina's case, the whiskey hadn't hurt.

When they hopped out of the car and slammed the door behind them, he remembered how he used to scold them for that. Now he just whistled, making plans in his head that included them. Hiking in the Zagoria in waterproof boots, movies in Syntagma, loafing around the house on Sunday mornings eating Her pancakes. Plans come more easily in cars. There's the forward momentum, the miles slipping by, the hope that somehow you'll break free. During his first years with Her, they literally lived in the car. They talked in the car, ate in the car, embraced, dozed, watched the raindrops breaking against the windshield. She was working in the real estate office by then, but still living with her parents. And he was living with his wife and kids. Hotels struck him as cold, impersonal places.

They hadn't exactly decided to move in together. Her parents decided for them, by sending tapes of their telephone conversations to his house, with all those breathless I-miss-yous and What-are-you-wearings. His wife had listened to the tapes in the living room, with the girls. She was sitting in her wheelchair—not the electric one she had now, but an older, manual model—and couldn't kick anything to let out her rage. So she squeezed her hands together, so hard that her pinky finger broke. He found his suitcases waiting for him in the hall. Ever since then no one had wanted to see him or hear news of him. He became just that, "He." They used his new name perfunctorily, in sentences like, "He called," or "He can go to hell for all I care."

"Since you didn't want to take care of Mom anymore, you're not really, not really . . ." Stella had suddenly said on their way toward the parking lot in Syntagma. The light was fading and he couldn't see her face. Christina had stopped at a kiosk and he and Stella stood there waiting for her. Neither of them spoke until his younger daughter opened her mouth and started to stammer.

"Go on, say it," he encouraged.

"You're not really good. I thought you were good."

He kicked at a crushed soda can that lay on the ground by his feet.

"Everyone's good," he said. "We're all good."

"But it's awful to abandon someone who's disabled."

"It's awful to leave, however you do it. Things were over between your mother and me a long time ago."

"You should have sacrificed yourself."

"I did."

"We sacrifice ourselves every day."

"That's bad for her, and bad for you, too."

Stella shook her head as if she wished he would suck the words back into his mouth. Christina came up to them holding a lit cigarette. She took a deep drag. She had flipped up the collar of her raincoat. She looked determined and fateful.

"Does anyone want a cigarette?" she said.

"I quit."

"You quit?" Christina asked shrilly. "Did She make you?"

"You two need to realize, She's not holding a knife to my neck."

"She's bewitched you, Dad," Stella said.

Just then all the streetlights came on at once and he saw the tears brimming in his younger daughter's eyes.

By then they had reached the parking lot and it had started to rain again. They busied themselves with more practical matters. Keys, money, where the girls were going to sit. In the end Christina sat up front and Stella in back. The whole way home Stella stared out the window, and when they arrived she stuck her head between the two front seats. She patted him on the back and he turned around to give her a kiss.

"Stella . . ." he said.

Christina was wheeling around outside the car, enjoying her drunkenness.

"Yes?"

"I want you to try to have faith in your own opinions. Don't let yourself be influenced by Christina or your mother. Or by me."

She smiled confidently and stepped out of the car, sending him something between a wave and a kiss.

He watched her as she wiped her galoshes on the doormat in front of the apartment building. Her legs were symmetrical, bony and thin, like the legs of the bar stool she'd been sitting on a short while ago.

The driver of the car behind him was honking like mad.

An hour later he stood on the doormat of his own apartment building, wiping the mud from his shoes, hunched over to avoid the sharp leaves of the palm tree that had bowed down under the weight of the rain. He was proud of the apartment they had found on a steep side street in the suburb of Vrilissia, where all of Athens lay stretched out beneath them. The only problem was that their road flooded whenever it rained. The asphalt kept forming potholes, and a truck would come and repave it badly, so they lived all winter long in a mud flat with palm trees—a miserable oasis. He stepped into the elevator, looked at himself in the mirror, and abruptly stopped whistling. His worst self was staring back at him: yellow, with blue lips and black circles under his eyes. He kept forgetting to tell the super to change the light bulb in the elevator.

She was waiting for him on the sofa, in a caftan with little mirrors all over it. She had her feet tucked under the cushion and was looking over a stack of blueprints.

"Sell anything today?" he asked, tired.

"I've got no complaints," She said, smiling. "How about you?"

"Me . . . I don't want to do anything. Just to watch."

"You're tired."

"No, it's more serious than that. I'm cursed."

"We've said all this before. We can live with it."

"Sometimes it's hard."

"I know."

He loosened his tie, poured himself a shot of vodka, and drank it down straight, in a single swallow. It was his fourth or fifth drink of the evening, and it had an unexpected effect. The lighted windows in the buildings outside the balcony door stretched and swayed. *The firefly hunt is beginning*, he said to himself. He was always surprised by these alcohol-induced thoughts, the ones that resemble riddles. He sank down beside Her on the sofa and closed his eyes. Even the darkness was spinning.

"One minute they were so harsh with me, and the next they were acting as if they'd forgotten all about it."

"Isn't that human?" She said, unbuttoning his cuffs. "We all want to forget."

"You think?"

"Sometimes I dream that I met you first, that you'd never even met her at all."

"That's not very realistic," he said. "What would I have done all those years, waiting for you to finish school?"

She rested her head on his shoulder and slipped her hand up his sleeve to stroke his elbow. One of the mirrors on her dress scratched a vein. *My little fireflies*, he thought again. *They glow for an instant and then . . .*

"I think I might turn in early tonight," he said to her.

"I'll be in soon."

While he was undressing it struck him that She hadn't really asked him for a detailed account of the meeting, the way women usually do. She was so discreet that sometimes he thought her unfeeling. In his universe women were always asking endless questions about everything. But this way the meeting could remain almost entirely his own. He could brood on it in the darkness.

He pictured his girls perched on their barstools, in their black clothes and with that light in their eyes. He closed his own eyes and pulled his daughters deep inside of him, where no one could take them away.

Teef

"Would you like to discuss the next case?"

She's standing over me, blocking the ray of light that would otherwise stream through the window and warm the stapler, the legal pads, the plastic surfaces of the computer, and my arms. It's a rhetorical question. "Would you like" is just a manner of speaking, a phrase that she's learned to use. Her doctoral dissertation was on "Will and the Superego."

My supervisor is an ordinary woman. She reminds me of the leader we had in my girl scout troop when I was little. Our troop leader, too, wore mannish, lace-up shoes of soft leather and calf-length woolen skirts. Her hair, brown and unruly, was always escaping from some supposed bun. There was a faint moustache on her upper lip, just as there is on my supervisor's.

On nice days she suns herself by the window, keeping one eye on things, like a cat. Her office is the best and biggest on the floor. It has a view down into the yard of the mental health facility where we work. When the weather is nice, like today, healthy visitors stroll through the yard with sick patients, like people taking their dogs for a walk. And the patients often resemble animals. They express sadness or wild joy the same way dogs do.

Whenever I go in to leave an evaluation on my supervisor's desk, I always stand for a while looking down into the yard. I like the pine tree, with its strong, swollen trunk. The patients all seem drawn to it, too, as if it offers some kind of advice or serves as an example to them, in the way it grips the soil so fiercely, with all of its roots. As for me, it makes me remember episodes from my camping days, when we'd collect dry branches for kindling and cross ourselves before bed on our knees in front of our cots. Our troop leader would tell us some didactic story about the importance of protecting the weak, and the world would become a heroic place. My present-day troop leader doesn't tell parables, but when she leans over me and asks if I'd like to discuss the next case, that old flame flickers.

In the language of psychiatry, patients are called cases. And though I'm learning to see them that way, like classified cases of neurotic or psychotic behavior, the terminology is still painful. It cuts to the bone. Especially if you're a graduating senior like me, torn between clinical terminology and emotional investment. Emotional investment—another odd turn of phrase.

Our discussions go as follows: my supervisor talks, and I, silent, take notes on a legal pad. My pen scratches the paper aggressively—noises like that are permitted. During consultations with a case, students don't interfere. They sit in a chair in the corner of the room, staring down at their papers or their watch as if they were waiting for a bus.

"As you like," I answer.

We both know we're using the language affectedly, exaggeratedly. Our conversations sound like dialogues from a TV series or a book on manners.

"Today we'll go to see the woman on the stretcher."

I let out a little cry. The woman on the stretcher is one of the Untouchables. That's how we students refer to the cases we don't ever get to see, because they're considered complicated, and, in a way, atypical. I myself would call them magical cases, but we're required to shed any non-scientific approaches at the door.

"Perhaps you would prefer not to see that case?" my supervisor asks, narrowing her eyes. I don't know whether to attribute it to the sun or to her insidious irony.

"On the contrary. I'm honored by your trust in me."

This is something else that we both know well: our courtesy is contractual, and has no emotional import. We pretend that it does.

"Now where are those papers . . ." she says, rifling through a few drawers.

While she's searching, I think about the woman on the stretcher. She shows strong signs of autism and is being treated on the top floor, in the Forbidden Zone. On warm days two nurses bring her down to the yard on a stretcher, which they leave resting on the roots of the pine tree. The woman squirms under her sheet, throws off the blanket, waves her arms and legs, lets out inarticulate cries. I watch from the supervisor's window: for hours on end she acts as if she has no spine whatsoever. She rolls from the stretcher onto the grass, flips onto her stomach, struggles to lift her head, then starts to cry. It's something I've only seen newborn cats do. Until the nurses come to pick her up, I cover my ears. My right hand shakes.

"Here, look this over," my supervisor says, handing me the woman's file. "We'll pay her a visit after lunch."

I'm happy, just as I was when my troop leader let me gather wood all by myself and arrange it in the fire pit. The pine gave off a heavy scent of pitch, night fell slowly to the soil, and I felt responsible for the light—like a kind of torch bearer.

I open the file and become engrossed in its contents. The woman on the stretcher is thirty years old. She was born in Thessaloniki and came to Athens to study economics. She got a job at a real estate agency, where she met her future husband. He was married at the time, with two girls. The divorce was a matter of months, as was their decision to make a new start together. They rented an apartment behind Venizelos Park. She busied herself with buying furniture and fixing up the apartment. She put a lot of thought into the upholstery, trying to pick the perfect shades. Every day she would cook something new and inventive. She was a perfectionist. The best worker at the agency, the best housewife, the best surrogate mother for the two girls who came to live with them. Soon a third child was born into the house. The woman on the stretcher considered doctors superfluous: with the help of a midwife she pushed a healthy baby boy out into the world.

Every morning she woke up when her son did. She held him to her breast and spoke to him in whispers. She changed him, kissing his belly, smoothing moisturizer into the folds of his skin. She made up pet names for him and sang to him. She took him on walks in his stroller and pointed out trees, cars, dust-covered flowers. She watched for cracks in the sidewalk, and so the baby wouldn't take fright she said, "Oopsie daisy," before every sudden dip.

The problems began in the baby's fourth month, when he started to produce his first inarticulate babbling noises. Impressed by the deep vowels and the gurgling consonants, the woman on the stretcher started to mimic the sounds. She would sink her face into the baby's neck and repeat whatever he said: *aeg, ki ka, hhhhhhhh, ma ma ma.*

One day her husband came home and found her lying in the baby's playpen, playing with the mobiles hanging from the ceiling. She showed him how the bright yellow rattles and singing frogs spun around their own axes. Her husband stood for a minute in the door. *He was impressed*, my supervisor had noted, *by his wife's ability to play freely, like a child. In similar situations, he himself always felt inadequate and ridiculous.*

These instances of erratic behavior became gradually more frequent. The woman on the stretcher would suddenly burst into laughter or tears. She would stare at her fingers. She would spend countless hours lying in bed, the baby in her arms. She soon lost herself in those sounds—her linguistic capacity diminished, then vanished altogether. At first she forgot individual words. She would say, "Can you bring me that," pointing to a glass or to her shoes. Then she started to break words in half and toss out the second part, or cut a syllable from the middle. Skirt became ski. Underwear became unear. Around that time her legs bowed outwards. The bones at the top of her skull separated, forming a soft little ditch in the center.

Meanwhile her skin turned rosy, her freckles disappeared, her toenails softened and peeled. She was more beautiful than ever. Her husband confessed that not even during their first clandestine encounters—when he was still married to his first wife and never imagined that this young woman would one day be his—had she been so cool and fresh. Lying on the bed, she would smile at him, and from her lips would flow a stream of vowels, or a spurt of saliva. Her teeth fell out. She chewed on her son's brightly-colored rattle to ease the pain.

She was brought here when she could no longer sit up on her own. They called her "the woman on the stretcher" and attached sidebars to her bed so she wouldn't fall off. Her son was raised by his father alone. His half-sisters wouldn't play with him, a fact that would have wounded the woman on the stretcher. But by now she was in no position to judge. She lived for the smell of rice flower and baby powder. Her only responses to her environment were a reflective laugh and a robust cry.

"Where is this all heading?" I wondered out loud. I wanted to hear the sound of my voice, so as to feel less alone.

The light in my supervisor's office was dancing, taking the shape of the thick dust in the air. I had apparently been affected by the woman's story: I was seeing the sun not as a given, but as an optical game. Then I curled up in a fetal position in the chair and tried out a little cry.

I was afraid whatever she had might be contagious. I squared my shoulders decisively and ordered the papers into piles.

My supervisor's footsteps echoed rhythmically in the hall, like a wind-up toy.

"Shhh. Don't say a word. I came so we could talk a little."

The woman on the stretcher smiled.

"You understand everything, don't you? You chose to do it, all on your own. Only now you've strayed so far that you need help to get back. Back to us, I mean—to the real world."

The woman on the stretcher smiled again and said, "Tttt-HHHHH."

"They're stupid rationalists, all of them. They think treatment means drugs."

"TtttHHHHH."

I took the bottle out of my jacket pocket.

"I brought you a little ouzo," I said. I lowered the sidebar on the bed, lifted her head, and put the bottle in her mouth. "It's good for a toothache."

She sucked greedily and burped.

"You like it, huh? Of course you do."

Outside my supervisor's window, the big pine tree yielded to the wind. And I yielded to the orders I was given. Willingly, not fatalistically. Winter was coming and my daydreams dwindled, along with the visitors. The first cold snaps awoke in me the desire to help. I was still just a little girl scout who wanted to save lame dogs and learn how to light fires without burning the whole forest down. I went up to the Forbidden Zone and gently turned the key in the lock. The woman on the stretcher greeted me with a "ttttHHHHH." It must mean "thank God." Or something like that.

"Is it nice being a kid? I mean, you'd know better than any of us. Don't pretend you don't understand!"

Today she was annoying me. I grabbed the baby bottle full of wine and took two big swigs.

"Teef," she said.

"What?"

"Teef."

She opened her mouth to show me the little seeds of her new teeth.

"Congratulations!" I said. "You're growing up."

"Mmmmmm," she said.

"I don't care if you talk or not. I just care that you understand."

The woman thought about what I had said, gulping my words down greedily with her wine.

Another day I told her, "Sometimes when I see little babies playing in the park, standing up and falling back down, eating dirt, I'd like to . . ."

"Mmmmmm," she said.

". . . roll around with them, too, you know? But I stop myself, I close that tap tight."

"Mmmmmm."

"I know how it is. Sometimes I don't want to do anything. Just to watch."

"Yes."

She'd said her first yes.

"Were you jealous?" I asked, trying not to look at her.

She stuck out her hand and grabbed the bottle. She could drink by herself now.

The supervisors were so pleased with themselves. They all believed her improvement was a result of the drugs they had prescribed. Whenever my supervisor would stand there with the others discussing her case, the deep desire would gnaw at me, all the way to the bone, to tell them the truth. It was getting dark early these days, and in the afternoons when they would stand in front of the window, slowly stirring their coffee with little spoons, their profiles would harden until they looked like transparencies stuck to the glass. I would drop whatever I was doing, make some excuse, and sneak up to her room. I'd hide a baby bottle of ouzo or wine, cigarettes, and vanilla-scented room spray in my pockets. I'd rest my chin on the sidebar of the bed and talk to her. Or I would read to her from Rilke:

I believe that almost all of our sadnesses are moments of spiritual tension, which we experience as a kind of paralysis, terrified because we feel that our startled emotions are no longer living, that we have been left alone with the foreign thing that has entered us, deprived of everything to which we were tied by bonds of habit and trust, that we are standing in the midst of a transition where we cannot stand much longer. And that is why the sadness passes: the New, the Unknown enters us, makes its way into the innermost recesses of our heart, and even moves on from there, running now in our blood. We could easily be convinced that nothing has happened, and yet we have changed, as a house changes when a stranger enters it. Only we cannot say who has entered; that we will never know.

The woman would nod and take a drag or two of my cigarette. The moon painted her bald head with a layer of silver. The first hairs were sprouting there like mastic leaves.

"What right did you have?" my supervisor asked.

As usual, I glanced down at the pine tree.

"I asked you something."

"I have no excuse," I said.

"Do you understand what this means for your career?"

I smiled at the pine tree.

"So that doesn't concern you?"

"I'm only concerned with her progress. And—"

"And you're such a megalomaniac as to believe that her progress is due entirely to your intervention?"

"I'm leaving anyhow."

"Of course you're leaving. This instant. Go and collect your things."

The whole time I was emptying my locker I could feel her frozen breath on my back.

"We're packing up and getting out of here," I whispered.

Her eyes flew open and she opened her mouth to scream. I covered it with my hand.

"Shhh, that's the last thing we need. Either we leave together or I'm leaving alone."

The woman sat up. She could sit up now. Her four new teeth shone in the dark.

"They're kicking me out. It's your only chance."

"Huh?" she said.

"Are you coming?"

She nodded her head frantically.

"Yes, yes, yes," she said.

"Do you remember what Rilke said about the absorption of our fate?"

"Yes, yes, yes," she said.

"Are you going to be able to walk?"

She puckered her lips and scrunched up her face to cry.

"There's no time for that now."

I lowered the sidebar and helped her sit on the edge of the bed. Her feet touched the floor.

"Try to remember how to walk."

She stood up, leaning on the sidebar, then fell into my arms.

"Try to remember. We have to at least get to the elevator."

I took off my beige scarf and wrapped it around her head, covering her sparse hair. Wearing that kerchief she looked like a baby who had grown old, a woman of no discernable age.

"Now we need shoes. Do you remember shoes?"

"Yes, yes, yes."

Dressed in her old clothes she looked like one of those big dolls that people used to have in their living rooms, the kind with perfectly smooth skin, without any of the wrinkles that give a face an expression.

"Come on, one step at a time. What does Rilke say? *Tomorrow stands motionless, as we move tirelessly into an infinite expanse.*"

She smiled, took a step, and fell excited into my arms.

The corridor was empty and cold, like the inside of a fridge. But when I opened the door of the elevator, we were surrounded by a soft yellow light.

"Don't give up now."

She was lying exhausted on the grass. I was pulling her by the ankles. The wind was raging. The pine tree was waving at us with all of its branches. I unlocked the front gate and dragged her a little further, to the car. I opened the passenger's side door and helped her in, then fastened her seat belt.

"We've almost done it . . ."

I put up the collar on my coat and pointed to the gaping hole in the roof.

"We've got a great air conditioner, see?"

"Mmmmm."

"Once my sister got into a fight with my mom. She took the car and drove it into a tree. She didn't get hurt, but the roof caved in. She had them tear off the whole top. When it rains, she gets rained on. When it's cold, she freezes. That way she remembers."

The first drops of a light, uneven rain fell on our hands, in our faces. I put the key in the ignition.

"Do you know what my sister says? Rain is something that happens inside of us. If it rains for enough people, then we see rain. Otherwise—"

"Oh," said the woman.

I looked where she was looking. A cold white light poured down on us.

"Would you please step out of the car?"

The night watchman was patrolling the corner. He must have approached us quietly, with his flashlight off. Now he was shining it down on us through the missing roof.

"No, no, we're not coming in, not now. I just wanted to show my mother the clinic."

"Your mother?"

"Could you please turn off that flashlight? The least little thing can set her off."

"What are you doing here?"

I rolled down my window. He bent down and continued to scrutinize us. I hadn't seen him before. He must have been new.

"I'll tell you again," I sighed. "I'm looking for a clinic for my mother. She's gotten old and can't take care of herself anymore."

"Why didn't I see you driving in?"

"For Christ's sake, I came around the other way! I switched off the headlights before I parked. She's afraid of people—and of lights, too. We drive around each night looking for a place she might like."

"This place is nice," he said, lighting a cigarette.

"Yes, and there's a big courtyard, from what I see."

"But it's not a nursing home. To get in here you need . . . you know, to have a screw loose somewhere."

"We're all a little crazy."

"What do you say, lady, you like it here?" he asked, waving his flashlight. It was big and black. It looked like a crowbar.

"Mmmmm."

"Sorry, I didn't understand. Do you like it or not?"

She opened her mouth and pointed to her four brand new teeth.

"Teef," she said, after a struggle.

"Extractions," I explained. "The way things are going she'll be completely toothless before long."

"You should get her dentures. My mom wears dentures."

"Well, goodnight," I said, and turned the key in the ignition.

"What happened to your car?"

"It's a long story."

I sped off down the dirt road, watching as he got smaller and smaller in the rearview mirror, until he finally disappeared.

The light of the moon escorted us as we drove. It was the flashlight of some other being, formless and gray, that breathed rhythmically over our heads.

Overcome

I let the cold water run. I tried to prop up the bouquets between the cases of beer, but a few flowers escaped and floated around in the bathtub. We had run out of vases. Out of dessert spoons, too. I should have gone back into the kitchen to let someone know, but instead I knelt down and began to stroke the water, gently at first, then more and more forcefully, creating a little whirlpool in the tub. Then I dried my hands on a towel and went out of the bathroom. I was afraid I might start crying.

You can tell how old someone is by the smell of his urine. Before flushing I breathed in deeply, inhaling my age. The water swirled up around the sides of the basin, and the toilet bowl freshener my wife bought let out a whiff of sea breeze. Is that what I am? An old man on a chemical beach? I washed my hands thoroughly and dried them on my worn corduroys. I thought of her hands.

I kissed the newcomers on the cheek. I put their gifts in the room with the gifts, their coats in the room with the coats. Some of them wanted to know where the bathroom was, others where the drinks were, and still others wanted, standing there in the hall, to tell me how happy they were for us, squeezing my hands in theirs as proof of the magnitude of their joy. And since they were all asking and talking and squeezing at once, I got flustered, and thanked someone who was looking for the drinks, and told someone else, who was shaking my hand and asking me how I felt, "Through the kitchen, second door on the right."

In the hall I bumped into Perky's water bowl. "We'd better put this out of the way," I said. My wife was cooking in the kitchen. Her hips moved with the rhythm of the mixing spoon. It occured to me that the female body mixes the male body thoroughly, until it softens. "We'd better put this out of the way," I said again. The noise from the exhaust fan drowned out my voice. I blew my nose into a tissue.

I poured myself a glass of whiskey and drank it down. Right away the truth of things began to shine on the curtains and the reflective surfaces in the room. I could always just become an alcoholic, to get away from all this.

"Did I step on you, dear?" Mom asked. She knelt down and smeared saliva onto a scratch on my ankle. "But look at you, in the middle of . . ." She let her sentence trail off, studying me more carefully, with a parent's pathological worry, the kind that makes you want to take another swig, straight from the bottle. She shook her head several times. "You're tired, honey," she said.

"What did you say?" my wife asked.

"Nothing. I was just blowing my nose." I took another tissue. I blew, coughed, spat, blew again.

"You're still in bad shape, huh?"

"Awful. What are you making?"

"Soup."

Soup. The perfect thing for anyone who doesn't feel able-bodied or secure, who goes soft just watching the cyclical motion of a mixing spoon. I thought of her hands again, and of Perky's wet nose. I peered over my wife's shoulders and saw potatoes, carrots, onions, and a soup bone.

"Could you maybe take out the bone?"

"Sorry, I wasn't thinking," she said, and fished it out with a slotted spoon. When she opened the lid of the trash can, my eyes grew heavy with tears that refused to flow.

"I'm fine," I told Mom. As soon as I said it, I began to feel better. I poured myself another whiskey and started to wander from room to room, shaking hands, giving orders to the help. I stuck two bottles of pink champagne in the bathtub with the flowers and the beer. "Move over, I know you'll fit."

Just then my husband stuck his head around the door. He was holding the cordless phone in his hand, saying to someone, "Great, we'll talk soon." He put the phone down on the little shelf with the soaps and creams and sighed.

"Have you lost it, too?" he asked.

We sat silently on the side of the tub. The only thing that spoke was the second hand of his watch, asking, what, what, what, what, what?

"Why are you covering your ears?" he asked.

"I can't stand the sound of your watch."

Then he did something very romantic, something I would have thought only one man in the whole world was capable of doing: he loosened the band of his watch, took it off, and tossed it into the tub. "Don't cry," he said. "It's waterproof."

"Don't cry. I can't stand it when you cry," my wife said. "Just think how old she was. It had to happen sooner or later." She spoke slowly and sadly over the boiling soup, her words taking on an aphoristic quality, like dialogue in dreams.

"I dreamed about her this afternoon, you know, while I was napping."

"What was she doing?"

"She was digging a hole in the ground with her front paws. And water was gushing out of the hole amazingly fast. Like a fountain."

"Sounds nice . . ."

I assured him I was fine, the guests were just getting on my nerves; weddings are so draining, particularly when they're yours.

"So we're married. We really did it, huh?" he said. He smiled tiredly and hugged me so tightly my bones creaked.

"I don't want to do anything. Just to watch . . ."

"That'll happen. Be patient. It'll all happen."

He grabbed a bottle of pink champagne by the neck, then headed for the kitchen. I closed the door behind him, picked up the cordless phone from the shelf and started playing with its little number keys. I didn't know whether or not I was going to call. The phone was still warm from my husband's hand. I had promised myself that this whole story would end.

"Nice? What's so nice about it?"

"I see it as a promise of life. You know, the fountain that washes away all the badness . . ."

"There is no such fountain," I said.

"Of course there is." She said it persuasively, with a conspiratorial air. The old love wrapped itself around us, the steady love we had gotten used to trusting in. A love without needs, without bodies, without recompense.

"I wonder . . ." I said.

"What?"

"I wonder if you're the fountain."

What's the harm in a few innocent lies? Besides, there's no fountain anymore, no wasteful extravagance, no drive for something higher—so why not?

"Oh, you," she said, and gave me a hug.

It's strange how that happens, when you're in pain: the person you're closest to has no body anymore, just a spiritual presence, and there are moments of such complete osmosis, such familial accord, that you could almost turn to her and say, "I'm in love with a girl who got married today."

My mind screams out that phrase. The soup echoes it with its boiling. The cooking hood sucks it up.

My wife moves off, shaken.

"Well, let's eat, before it gets cold," she says.

I sat down on the bathroom rug and played for a while with the number keys on the phone. The closed door blocked the sounds of the music. The laughter and conversation droned on with the intensity of a low-grade complaint.

I wanted to see how you were doing. Fine, fine. I was worried about the dog, is she better? I'm glad. I knew everything would be fine, you'll see.

But no matter how many times I rehearsed it, I was afraid things wouldn't be fine at all.

I dialed mechanically, as if punching numbers into my calculator at work, some sum that just refused to come out right.

My wife was opening and closing cupboards and drawers, taking out spoons, napkins, plates, the salt and pepper shakers. I unfolded the blue checked tablecloth. It made a disturbing rustling noise in the air before falling to cover the tabletop. We sat down and stirred our hot soup. The steam licked my cheeks, my nose, my chin.

"It'll help with your fever, too," my wife said.

"I know."

I tasted a bit of soup from the tip of my spoon, smacking my lips. Life is so much simpler when you're with someone you can blow your nose and smack your lips in front of.

The telephone rang.

"Don't get up," I said. "I'll get it."

The light from the cordless phone blinked on and off in our dark hallway.

"I wanted to see how you were doing," she said.

He didn't answer so I said it again, more loudly, "I wanted to see how you were doing."

He coughed.

"Do you have a cold?"

"Yes."

"I wish I were with you. I'd make you some tea."

"I'm eating soup. A really wonderful soup."

I'd interrupted their dinner. It was something I used to do often, with the pleasant sensation of being in control.

"Sorry for calling during dinnertime."

He laughed, then coughed, and I could tell he was taking the phone into another room, because one door closed and another opened, and then he said, with a sigh, "I'm alone now. How was the wedding?"

"Fine. Like a wedding."

"Meaning?"

"What do you want to hear? That I got all choked up and cried?"

He didn't answer.

"How's Perky?"

"Gone."

"You mean . . ."

"Yes."

"What happened?"

"She started spitting blood. We took her to the vet, but it was too late."

"My God!" I said, and then we didn't say anything for a while. He coughed a few times, and I started making circles in the water with my free hand.

"You should get back to your guests," he finally said.

"Thanks for calling me to order."

"Order came on its own. I didn't do anything. I'm just trying to maintain it."

"There's no order anywhere. Anywhere."

"I'm sure it'll take some time for us to see the results."

I wiped my hand on my sugar-colored dress and mentally prepared myself to say something. But suddenly everything was right, soft, reasonable. Everything flowed around me gently.

"I wanted to see how you were doing," she said again, stressing the words.

I coughed. I'd gotten into the habit of changing the subject, to avoid these awkward moments.

"Do you have a cold?" We started talking about tea and soup and she apologized for interrupting our dinner. Then I realized that my wife was at the end of the hall and started walking with the cordless phone in my hand. I went into my office and sat down at my desk. It was covered with used tissues.

"Now I'm alone. How was the wedding?"

"Fine. Like a wedding."

"Meaning?"

"What do you want to hear? That I got all choked up and cried?"

I didn't answer.

"How's Perky?"

"Gone." It's a word that could apply to so many things.

"You mean . . ."

"Yes."

"What happened?"

"She started spitting blood. We took her to the vet, but it was too late."

I didn't want to go into all the details, because Perky would start writhing again on the vet's metal table.

"My God!" she said.

"You should get back to your guests," I said, then coughed again to fill in the silence.

"Thanks for calling me to order," she said.

"Order came on its own. I didn't do anything. I'm just trying to maintain it."

"There's no order anywhere. Anywhere."

I told her it would take a little time for us to see the results. I looked at the used tissues and thought, There's something you'll never see—real life slips away when we lie down on a bed in some hotel and I stroke your face for hours on end. And if we get tired of being good, I pull your hair until your neck arches back and you give in. We don't make a big deal of it.

"You know I want to see you," I said. "Don't torture me."

I heard a thump, as if she'd dropped the phone on the floor.

"She's overcome," someone said.

They were all hanging from the ceiling. In the time it took for the floor to return to its proper place I had a chance to think things through. I had dialed the numbers one by one, I had spoken with him. I'd imagined him eating his soup, each spoonful offering him a taste of the end. Perky's death had upset him even more than our parting. Whenever he used to speak of the future he would say, "Get married, live your life, I'll take Perky on long walks, I'll be fine. We'll go up into the hills, to Penteli, and I'll let her off the leash and watch her run." I was more jealous of his dog than of his wife. I imagined him over a grave, crying. If I had died, he'd have been crying for me.

So I did the closest thing to dying: I fainted.

"Who was it?" my wife asked.

"No one. For me."

It was harsh, but I couldn't think of anything better. I had nothing left but myself and the certainty that we would keep opening and closing the front door and the floor in the hall would keep squeaking.

"Won't these telephone calls ever end?" she said, stirring her soup.

I spat a little bone into my napkin.

"They ended," I said.

"I'm not so sure."

You should be. I'm just an old man with bronchi full of phlegm and a hole in his chest.

I rubbed my chest over my heart, through the bridal gown. The rubbing reminded me of the way he used to touch me there: a circular motion. Mechanical, hysterical, hopeless. It used to excite me to be giving myself to a body half wasted from use. Isn't that what passion is? To be aroused by the idea of an unsuitable offering?

And yet I wanted that bridal gown. I needed a normal life in all its stages.

"Better now?" my husband asked. He pulled a rose from one of the bouquets in the bathtub and offered it to me.

I closed my eyes and inhaled.

Story for Fools

He yanks her, lifts her high, throws her down and she's gone.

From where she's gone, there's no coming back.

She likes it a lot or doesn't like it at all but either way she doesn't know how to leave so she stays. Time passes. For her, though, it doesn't pass; for her, time doesn't count.

No one knows what the difference is. They only know there's a big difference. There they don't sit, don't speak, aren't afraid.

And what if they are afraid?

What if they fall into a black hole and are constantly afraid?

How do we know?

He yanks her, lifts her high, throws her down and she's gone.

He's bad. He laughs while he's doing it.

She falls.

The moment when she's falling must be nice. But after that?

After that it won't be so nice.

It's raining and the people are getting wet. But no one leaves. They all want to know where she's gone. They form a circle around her. Is she still there? Or is she already gone? One of them is sure she's gone, and sure she won't be needing anything where she's going. He slips his hand into her coat pocket and pulls out her wallet.

He pulls out her red beret, too.

There you don't need a wallet, a hat, aspirin. Cookies, cigarettes, newspapers, whiskey.

And what if you do but no one will give them to you? How long would it take you to get used to a thing like that?

I can't go over to look. If they can steal her wallet they could rob me, too. The kiosk is full of useful things. If I could take it with me when I go, my business would skyrocket. They might not need the cigarettes, but they'd play with them. They would remember the crackling noise the plastic makes, the rustling of the foil, what it's like to smoke.

But do they know how to remember?

The police come and push the others aside. They want to see too. It's their job to look at such things. Why did they choose that job? To get used to seeing it? But it doesn't work that way. Better not to know anything, better for everything to come rushing at you all at once. Better that way than bit by bit.

The thief walks over to the kiosk. He asks for a pack of cigarettes without looking at me.

"You stole her wallet and her beret," I say, but I hand him the cigarettes because that's how it goes. It's none of my business where a man gets his money or what he does with it.

"I didn't steal them," he says. "I took them. It helps with the erasure. But how did you see?"

"With my eyes."

"You must be a very innocent man," he says. Then he lights a cigarette, blowing the smoke into the kiosk. When the cloud disperses I see that his eyes are yellow. I've never seen yellow eyes before.

"And the girl?" I ask.

"She was asking for it. She was looking for trouble."

"She wasn't a good person?"

"Everyone's good."

"You seem pretty wise. Do you know what it's like there?"

"Where?"

"Up there, down there . . ."

"In there, you mean?"

"You go in somewhere?"

"Way in."

"And what's it like?"

"I can't tell you."

"Tell me something. Just a little."

The man blows a puff of smoke again, this time toward the sky.

"It's like the kiosk," he says. "A little tight. But you've got everything right at your fingertips. You can touch it."

"Touch it?"

"If you want."

"You mean you don't want to?"

"Usually not."

"How come?"

"Because you're alone. There's no need to prove anything to anyone. You don't have an audience anymore, see?"

"You mean I'll be just like I am at home?"

"Exactly." His yellow eyes smile, pulling his mouth slightly open.

"What happened to your teeth?"

"They rotted. I've had to do some pretty strange things with my teeth."

"Such as?"

"You don't want to know."

The ambulance came while we were talking. They put her on a stretcher, covered her with a blanket, and slipped her in. Like the pan of half-eaten food we slip back into the oven for storage.

He yanked her, lifted her high, threw her down and she's gone.

"How can He stand to do that all the time?" I asked the man. He was lighting one cigarette after another, rubbing his yellow eyes whenever smoke got in them.

"What do you mean?"

"Kill them. Kill us."

"He likes blood."

"He's a murderer, you mean?"

"Once you start, you can't stop."

"Yeah, but how did it all get started?"

"He was born an old man, that's how it started."

"He had no parents?"

"Where would He have found parents?"

"He had a kid, though. That's something."

"Two kids."

"I only know about the one son."

"No, no, there were two daughters, Christina and Stella. Later on He remarried and had other kids, but we don't know too much about that part of His life."

"Remarried? You mean . . . He did it with women?"

"With just about anyone. He had a one-track mind. That's why the world is on the verge of collapse."

"And the girls' mother?"

"I can hardly remember . . . She was His first love. But then she got sick, disabled. She cried all day long . . ."

"Why did she cry?"

"He's not an easy guy to live with. He knows everything. He's always one step ahead of you."

"And He couldn't make her better?"

"When I say she was disabled, I mean on the inside. You can be God himself, but how are you going to fix that?"

"How should I know? I'm asking you."

"Well, what's really broken can't be fixed. We learned that when Christina died."

"Christina was the older daughter?"

"You mean you don't even know that?"

"But she was resurrected later."

"Bullshit she was resurrected. Her sister saw her coming down in a halo of light. He swallowed that story because He wanted to. And since He swallowed it, everyone else did, too."

"You're saying He'd lost it?"

"I wouldn't let Him hear me talking like that if I were you."

"You mean . . . ?"

"Why, what do you think?"

"That He's good."

"Of course He's good. Everyone's good."

"And what are you? His servant?"

"You could put it like that."

"Do you like that life?"

"I don't like anything. I don't fit in anywhere."

"But why are you telling me all this? Aren't you afraid that . . ."

"What was that? You're so innocent."

"That's what everyone says."

"You're so innocent that if you go on saying things like that they'll probably lock you up in an asylum."

"They did that once."

"I figured."

The man touched the index finger of his right hand to his temple, to suggest that it's best to think logically. Then he raised his eyebrows and turned around. His shoulderblades were sharp and pointed. They made two little lumps under his jacket.

My mind was stuck.

How could He do that job?

A girl with a red beret.

She could've been His daughter.

He yanked her, lifted her high, threw her down and she's gone.

I'd Like (Orchestral Version)

"I don't know where to start. Help me."

"How? I don't know what you want to say."

They're sitting up front. Snickering.

"Okay, fine. Let's get serious."

"The thing is . . ." He clears his throat. Fakes a cough.

"I don't want to hurt you, or lie to you," she says. "Don't take it the wrong way."

"You wanted us to tell you the truth, right?"

You're sitting in the back seat, and with the tip of one of your rain boots you push at the mat at your feet, lifting it up, then letting it drop. Again and again, until it finally tears. Something of theirs had to tear. If you were a dog you would rip them apart with your teeth. But you're a girl. Nineteen years old. The kind of girl who takes things out on the floor mats of cars.

"We read it carefully," she says.

"Very carefully."

"We marked all the syntactical mistakes, the exaggerations, the factual errors."

"The thing is, you'd have to change so much, that . . ."

"Better just to forget this one. Start from scratch. Learn to write."

She's your older sister. And in the passenger's seat, her new boyfriend. Tall, predictable, her shadow. Round glasses, checked shirt with snaps, smelling of unfiltered cigarettes, the usual stubble. They're both fourth-years in the Modern Greek Department at the University of Ioannina. Fortunately they didn't get into the University of Athens. Just imagine if you had to see them every day after this. To say hello.

"Can you give me an example?"

They look at one another. Their profiles take shape in the dusk. The curves of their noses and chins. Write about those curves. If you ever learn to write, that is.

"What's something specific?" your sister asks her boyfriend.

"Tell her what we were saying about the couple."

"Yeah, that's good. So they're supposedly a middle-aged couple, and when they meet the other couple, the famous writer and the famous artist, the wife has a nervous breakdown and runs off to Paris. That would never happen. Middle-aged people get over their ambitions, they settle. You're projecting. Those are a freshman's dreams."

The streetlight illuminates a circle of rain around it. The rest of the rain falls in darkness.

"What your sister is trying to say is that it's best to write about things you know."

Maybe you should put in some rain? Maybe the middle-aged woman could get rained on under a streetlight when she flips out? She's fifty. You know what it means to be fifty.

When he walks into the lecture hall you identify with him, you laugh when he laughs, you become him. You see something the others don't see: how afterward, at the hotel, you'll rest your head on his stomach and listen to him talking about stories he never dared to write, out of exaggerated respect for the ghosts of Voutiras and Vizyenos. You have no idea who Voutiras is. But he doesn't make fun of you—you've got time, he says. So to you middle age means tolerance, repressed dreams, the accretion of useless knowledge. Middle age has a soft belly that quivers almost imperceptibly and smells like an old hair band. And that thing in Paris actually happened to him. Once, before he met you, during a period of deep despair, he boarded a plane as if in a trance, as if following instructions, and landed at Orly. He wandered around Montmarte until dark. In the end he felt pathetic, sat down on a bench, and fell asleep.

"But the theme—" you stammer.

"It's trite. Besides, you should really leave it to people who know what failure means."

"I *do* know what it means."

"My dear," your sister says, adjusting the rearview mirror, "it's an entirely different thing to imagine that the whole world is devising sinister plans against you when you're a kid. That's part of what kids do."

Write, your dear, about a kid who suddenly grows up when she meets her adult self. The kind of kid who would suit a grown-up name. Stella, for instance.

"What your sister means, Stella, is that it's okay to talk about your own sadness."

They're translating for you, from Greek to Greek. Perhaps it's a solution. Stories for fools.

"Another example," she says. "Your title. 'I'd like'? I'd like? Please!"

"Why? It fits, in all kinds of ways."

You'd like this debacle to end, you'd like to find some excuse to leave. You'd like to have never shown it to her. What were you thinking? Of all the people in the world, her.

"That just means that it's easy. Don't rely on clichés."'

Try to communicate with them through something simple and true.

"I don't think it's a cliché. It's true. We'd all like something."

"So you're trying to evoke a particular emotional response. Come on, that's not an ethical stance."

"I'm not a thinker like you."

A thinker is someone who stifles. A feeler is the one who gets stifled.

"What you need is a balance between thinking and feeling," he puts in. "Algebra and fire, like Borges said."

"Forget Borges! That man is dangerous."

"Dangerous? Why?"

Great, they're talking about something besides you.

"Everyone imitates him. When people imitate you it means you're aiming for something that will sell. I mean, does anyone imitate Cavafy?"

"Sure. The authors of historical novels."

Please, let them fight . . . Let them fight and forget all about you. Years will pass, she'll become a lecturer at the university. Students will bring her papers they've written about your stories. He'll write book reviews. He'll push you down, you'll pick yourself up again, pull out the nails, push off the beams. Or maybe they could get jobs at a bank! They'd go home each night completely exhausted. You could give them each a few extra pounds, a dollop of despair, some sexual fantasies. And a baby that starts to cry whenever they finally manage to sit down with a book.

"Anyway. The real issue is your first short story. Not Borges or Cavafy."

Outside the car the rain pounds down. Inside, their words.

But there's a middle ground, too: the windshield wipers, which say what your sister doesn't dare say. Unimportant, fcht, unimportant, fcht, unimportant, fcht.

"What about me? Aren't you going to show it to me?"

His belly stiffens as he props himself up on his elbows.

"I'm never showing anything to anyone, ever again."

"You're insulting me."

"I'm not insulting you. I was in the car. I was the one who got insulted."

"Because your sister didn't like it? The sister who's always looking for ways to put you down? And that four-eyes who follows her around like a little puppy?"

He's said it just right. You lay your palms on his cheeks.

"Come here. You're freezing."

This cold is coming from within, but if you tell him that he'll take it personally. So you bury your head in the crook of his arm. Now you're alone with your thoughts and his body, running through the maze that's unfolding inside of you. You love him, but you know it won't last. He has kids, a wife, a house. You imagine him in that house. You imagine him spitting into the toilet, slurping his soup.

He has to have someplace where he can relax, and do all those gross things people do when they're alone.

"Come here, I said."

His voice gets hard and you know what he's really asking for. He flips you face-down, puts one hand over your mouth, and pulls your hair with the other. It's bizarre, but as long as you're in this world you like it. The ingenuity, the choreographed movements, even the bridle. *I'm a horse*, you think, *and I'm galloping*. Afterward, as if nothing out of the ordinary had happened between you, you sigh deeply and embrace.

"Do you know what I dreamed last night?"

"What?"

"That I called my house and talked to myself. There you go, there's the smile I love."

"What did you say to him?"

"I asked him what he was doing there and said he'd better be gone by the time I got back. The man who was supposedly me told me to fuck off and hung up on me."

Half with you, half at home. Did your father have dreams like that when he ran off with that little real estate agent? Little as in young, and little as in short, so ridiculously short. Next to your father she looked like an ant. There was a time when you thought your father was God, your mother was God's wife, and you two were their children. The world was created in a few years, then fell apart one afternoon when you sat together in the living room listening to the tapes. Then you went and did to some other family everything she had done to yours.

He moves your head aside to free his arm.

"Where are you sailing off to again?"

"I'm thinking about the dream you had. It would make a nice short story."

He smiles and starts putting his clothes back on.

"If you ever decide to write about a man talking to himself on the phone, you have my full permission."

The intensity fades and suddenly he's an old man again. You look at his belly, at his strange clothes, his thinning hair. His hair stays however he combs it, like muddy, ploughed rows in a field.

"Really. It'll be our little secret."

A ray of light slips through the shutters as you button your skirt. Sun after the rain. You'd like to be a speck of dust in that light, or a firefly. Something small, with no identity, so you wouldn't have to say, I'm sorry, I want to be alone now. So you wouldn't have to observe the proper order of things—going out with him into the street, kissing, making small talk to relieve the tension. The despair is all yours, and you want to enjoy it. To wrap yourself in it, like the kids wrapped in their windbreakers in your badly-written short story.

"Aspirin again?"

"Yep."

He smiles and hands you a box.

"You're not planning on killing yourself, are you? On taking them all at once? Death is no solution."

"Don't worry."

"I worry. I worry a lot. About you. About everyone, I mean, but especially you. So many people are dying . . ."

Sometimes you think he's your only real friend. He's always there, in the kiosk. He has all the literary magazines practically memorized. And he looks after you.

"The gum is on me. A gift, I mean. A gift from me to you."

He likes to say the same thing in lots of different ways. Maybe it's a nervous habit, or maybe he's got a screw loose somewhere.

"I don't chew gum."

"It's good for the mind. Repetition, I mean. Thinking about the same things."

You think about the same things anyhow, with or without gum.

"Did it really have to start raining again?"

"Are you worried your flight might be cancelled?"

"Please," she says, shaking out the sheet in front of the open balcony door. "I've told you my theory. Rain is something that happens in our heads. If it's raining for enough people, then we see rain. Otherwise it doesn't rain."

"I'll have to write that one down."

"Why?"

"Writers take notes."

"Writers?"

She doesn't look at you when she says it. She goes on making her bed, stretching the sheet smooth. Your skin feels stretched, too.

"I'm *going* to be a writer."

"Do you know how many people have said that?"

"What are you going to be?"

"I'll let life decide that for me."

Her bed is perfectly made. The gray bedspread has gone yellow from all the washings, but it's still sturdy, like an elephant's ear. How does she manage to imbue a stupid old bedspread with that much significance?

"Fatalism doesn't suit you, Christina."

"It's not fatalism to follow the flow. Fatalism is believing there's only one explanation for things."

"Is that a nail meant for me?"

"Nail? You live off metaphors. The only nail around here is the one that went into Mom's leg."

"Can I have a cigarette?"

"Since when do you smoke?"

You don't smoke. You just need to do something with your hands, with your unsteady breathing.

"Need a light, too?"

You lean forward, because the lighter is a good excuse to lean toward her. You light your cigarette and cough. Your eyes burn.

"Afraid I can't give you lungs to smoke it with. You'll have to use your own."

That was something that could only have come from her mouth. She has an entire arsenal of phrases like that.

"Okay, you didn't like the story, don't make a big deal out of it."

"But *why* didn't I like it?"

"You explained. I understood."

"I didn't explain. I didn't want to talk about such personal things in front of him."

"My story? Personal?"

"You think I'm an idiot? The wife who's an awful painter is Mom. And the husband who walks like an elephant is Dad. Instead of his being in advertising, you made him a failed writer."

"What do you mean?"

"A childless middle-aged couple. If they hadn't had us, they'd be dragging themselves along together just like that. Isn't that what you were implying, Stella? They would have been so busy worrying about their meaningless careers that they wouldn't have been looking for houses in the country, new curtains, stupid stuff like that."

"If you dig down deep enough in any story, you'll find an explanation of your own life. That's how it works. That's why we read books."

"But the question is, why do you want to write? Why shout out to the whole world what goes on in our house?"

"You're the one who told me to write about things I know!"

"I meant you should draw on your experience. Not turn our family into a newspaper column."

"So what should I have done, in your opinion?"

She sits down cross-legged on the wooden parquet. After all those years of ballet her joints open so wide that her knees practically touch the floor.

"Mix things up. Try putting the real estate agent in Mom's place."

"Why do you think I put that short woman, Pia Saunders, in a wheelchair?"

"You have to push things to extremes. Make her go crazy when she gives birth to that little brat. Make her hair fall out. Or her teeth."

"First of all, he's not a brat. He's our half brother. Besides, what do lies change?"

"What changes when a writer corrects an injustice? It shows that he cares about people!"

But you do care about people. You're your mother's personal nurse.

"Where's Mom?"

"In the kitchen. Eating ice cream out of the freezer."

"Not that again."

"Are you planning on writing about Mom, too? That'd be perfect. Pure melodrama."

Your mother will pass through all of your stories, stitching them together, working as discreetly and spitefully as always.

Your mother is like a jar of mustard that you open and then forget somewhere in the back of the fridge. Months pass before you discover it and feel sorry that it went wasted.

But she didn't go wasted.

She's the phantom of the fridge.

And Dad?

He's the phantom of the great outdoors.

"You're eating again?"

"Me? I was filling up the ice trays."

"Mom . . ."

"I'm not eating, honey. Why would I lie to you?"

Try to communicate with them through something simple and true.

"How was your day?"

"Just lovely! I met with my friends from the hiking club, stopped by a few galleries, and on the way home—"

"Mom!"

"What the hell do you want me to say? That's a question you ask healthy people."

"Do you want me to read you something?"

"Later. Thanks, but later."

She grapples with the wheels of her wheelchair. It's electric, but inside the house she prefers manual effort and struggle. The doctors say she could learn to walk again, if she would just take her physical therapy seriously. But then she'd lose all the advantages of self-pity.

She would have to act.

Your sister is packing her suitcase. She stuffs her cotton underwear with the little almond blossoms into the side pockets. She folds her clothes and lays them on the bottom. On top of them she stacks books, layer by layer, like bricks. As soon as she locks the bathroom door behind her, you run over to see what books she chose. *The End of Our Small City* by Dimitris Hatzis. *Writing Degree Zero* by Roland Barthes. The essays of Virginia Woolf. Poems by Maria Laina. Your hand accidentally brushes against her underwear and you shudder. Almond blossoms? She'd never just stand and admire a tree; she would shake it as hard as she could.

You used to spend hours together when you were little. You traded Smurfs. You played house under the dining room table, slurping invisible orangeades, serving invisible cake. She gave you her hand-me-downs. Cardigans that were so hers that when you put them on you smelled like her, walked like her. She would hug you so tight you thought you would break. And when she said "No," you would stop that instant.

But now you can't stop. The stories hatch in a place over which you have no control. In a landscape that reminds you of your dad's new house in the suburbs: mud, palm trees, and scaffolding. The workers sing old pop songs, dripping paint onto the sidewalk. On the news they say the neighborhood is undergoing a complete transformation, as the current owners sell their single-family homes to make way for new apartment buildings, new sapling trees, new trash bins on the streets. They're wasting their breath. Behind the new buildings, in a house made of plaster, the old cock will never die. He lives for the dawn, when he'll wake the whole neighborhood with his crowing.

"*Those around you are distant and aloof.*"

"Aloof? What's that?"

"Distant, detached. Should I go on?"

She stares at the curtain. She's disappearing again.

"Mom, should I go on?"

"Who did you say this guy was?"

"Rilke. Rainer Marie Rilke."

"Okay, keep reading."

"*Those around you are distant and aloof, you write—and that means that a great expanse is starting to open up around you, separating you from them. And if your surroundings are distant, that means the expanse is immeasurably vast, so vast it touches the stars. Take pleasure in the maturity you have gained, as something in which no one can follow you . . .*"

"Yeah, sure," she whispers.

"Mom, you keep interrupting."

"Are you trying to make me feel better? You're always choosing some baloney where people say one thing and . . ."

"*. . . and be good to those who stay behind,*" you continue, raising your voice just a notch. "*Be confident and calm before them. Don't trouble them with your doubts, don't frighten them with your zealotry or enthusiasm, for they wouldn't understand. Try to communicate with them through something simple and true.*"

"I'm tired," she says. "Let's stop."

"*Try to communicate with them through something simple and true.* Isn't that a great sentence?"

"You write much better."

"Oh, Mom, I read you Rilke and you—"

"It doesn't interest me, honey. It's armchair philosophy. You're better than any of them."

Better than any of them? In that immeasurably vast expanse you touch the stars, and the stars don't burn you because your own heat is hotter than anything in nature, hotter than anything that has yet been discovered by man. Your heat could burn fire itself.

"Are you giving her a swelled head again, Mom?"

She sticks her head into the doorway. She's holding her coat and a knitted red beret. She looks like a fox: reddish hair, sharp teeth, and that unique intensity in her gaze. You and your mother, the sheep, just sit there quietly chewing words.

"Do me the favor. I'm just saying what I believe."

"You don't know a thing about literature. So cut the crap."

"Watch your tongue, or I'll hand it back to you on a plate," Mom says, peering at Christina over her reading glasses.

"You think you know everything, huh? From how to cook a lamb fricassée to how to read books? Has it ever crossed your mind that you're stuck in your own stupid era, your stupid superstitions, your . . ."

She shouldn't have said stuck. Mom swivels around in her wheelchair. That means she's in despair, like a bolting horse.

"Just be glad you're going on a trip, because . . ."

"What? You're going to make my plane crash, you poor thing? What were you going to say? You're going to put a curse on me or something?"

"Shut up, both of you!"

Did that come from you? Cords are uprooted, your stomach rises into your throat.

"She's the one who should shut up!" Christina says.

She grabs the nearest object, a porcelain cat playing with a ball of yarn, and throws it to the floor. It smashes into a thousand pieces. There are dozens of glass figurines on the table and the cabinet. You can tell she's thinking of smashing them all, but in the end she just retreats into herself. She grabs her suitcase, drags it loudly across the floor. Ordinarily you would help her, you'd walk her out to the car, but right now you can't stand her calm dignity, the way she sweeps up everything in her path.

"Stella, I'm tough on you because you have to write well, or not at all."

"I don't want to write well, not the way you mean it. I just want to—"

"Go on, go on, get out of here," Mom says.

"Are you going to see me out?" your sister asks.

You don't answer.

She pulls the beret down to her eyebrows and disappears. The rolling of her suitcase echoes down the hallway, then in the street. The wheels squeak a lot, although the squeaking is coming from inside of you. There's some kind of gear caught in your throat, making it hard for you to breathe. The rain murmurs, Go to hell, go to hell. And the windshield wipers, unimportant, fcht, unimportant, fcht. The last thing you hear is the car door slamming. How many trips you all made together in that car, back when Dad was still driving it. How differently the windshield wipers squeaked then. And the rain fell gently, washing the landscape clean.

They call you a short while later. Unfamiliar voices speak incomprehensible words. She was speeding like an arrow toward the airport, she wasn't wearing a seatbelt. You see the roof of her car opening and pushing her outwards, upwards, into that immeasurably vast expanse, until she touches the stars. Then some stranger pulls her by her ankles to the stretcher. There isn't a scratch on her. Her coat and checked skirt rise up over her knees. And she doesn't curse him out, doesn't say, Take your dirty hands off me.

It didn't happen quite like that.

You fainted with the receiver in your hand.

Then you slept.

For a long time.

In the end, Mom did precisely what Christina had told her to: she shut up. If she needed anything she would point to it. Though she didn't need much anymore. She couldn't communicate with her surroundings, and couldn't take care of herself, so you put her in a mental health facility called the House of Serenity. Dad took care of everything.

And you? You lost your hair. It didn't matter, though. There was no one to see you like that, since you were shut up in the house, sleeping. Whenever you woke up you didn't want to do anything, just to watch. You stopped going to the university, didn't answer your professor's calls, didn't write another word. But you did read. Whenever you finished a really good book, your right hand would shake. You did a few book reviews for a small literary magazine. You, reviews. One day you found an abandoned puppy and brought him home. His fur was the color of burnt sugar, *zahari*, so you named him Zacharias. You abandoned reviewing in favor of love. Reading had become a nightmarish activity anyhow. More and more frequently, you would see your own thoughts printed on the page. You donated your books to the House of Serenity. The only ones you kept were Vizyenos, Foucault and Maupassant, tucked away in a box in the storeroom—they would have been bad for the patients. Whenever you felt a craving for some kind of story, you would read the ingredients on the cereal box, or the directions on a bottle of shampoo. You washed yourself constantly. A mild fear of microbes, the doctor said.

One rainy afternoon two boys came to your door. Their names shone on metal pins on their lapels. They listened to you, heard the sadness in your voice. They wanted to give you the Book of Mormon, an account of the life of Jesus Christ. You threw yourself into prayer. You, praying. Though in more simplistic words, their prophets said the same thing Rilke had written: *Love your solitude and endure, patiently but with a resonant complaint, the pain it causes you.* Christina would have insisted that Hatzis said it better: *It doesn't come on its own, my mind can't find it, and there's no one to give it to me.* You could hear her objections over the prayers. You asked the boys not to come again. Whenever you were overcome by the desire to believe in something, you would buy a big carton of ice cream and take it to the House of Serenity. Or you would go to the apartment in Vrilissia to see your little brother. His chubby hands, his saliva, the scent of milk, his picture books—those things helped. You were the big sister now.

What a role.

"Aspirin again?"

"What can I say . . ."

"You're not planning on killing yourself, are you? On taking them all at once? Death is no solution."

"I've heard that before somewhere."

"From me. Aspirin isn't gum, you know. If you want gum, take it. A gift. My treat."

"Thanks, but I don't chew gum."

"It's good for—"

"Thinking, I know. But I don't want to think."

"You have to think. How else will you write your reviews? Don't think I don't read what you write."

"Reviews? No, I stopped writing reviews."

"Why? They were the best reviews I've ever read. It was obvious how much you love books."

"That's the problem. I don't love books anymore."

"If you don't love books, who will? There's only a handful of us as it is."

"Don't take it to heart. I just read other things now."

You read deeds of purchase and parental transfers of property. Wills, detailed accounts of family quarrels, boundary disputes. You type quickly, but if you get stuck on a phrase, the sense of it gushes out like a fountain. The notary public is a family friend. If you linger too long, he just says gently, "Couldn't you do that a bit faster, dear?"

So you do it faster. Nowhere to be found, now, that immeasurably vast expanse that stretches to the stars. The sky is a black hole that sucks you in gently and empties you back out on the steps of your house. You feed Zacharias, you stroke his neck, and he rewards you with a yowl or two. You watch old super eights from family trips, hoping to find encoded meanings. But the only meaning is in the spinning: you and Christina and your cartwheel competitions.

At night in bed, you toss and turn until you finally drift off. In your dreams you see all the members of your family hanging upside-down from the sky like bats. Or stuck in a pile of whitish cement that turns out to be a huge, seething soluble aspirin. It dissolves in a colossal glass of water, and your parents and sister break free and rise to the surface, bursting with the bubbles. No one comes to save them. You wake up and go down into the kitchen, barefoot and panicked. Where does all the aspirin go? Your head hurts, like it used to with your professor. You shiver, as if someone, something, were touching you. You wrap yourself in a starched tablecloth, trying to stop the shivers. Zacharias hesitantly licks your foot. How long has it been since you held someone? Could you hold the man in the kiosk?

You close your eyes and think about the characters in your dreams. They all resemble you. They hug their knees to their chest; they touch objects warmed by other hands; they can't stand the ticking of a watch. They all resemble her, too. They love checked fabrics; they make their beds carefully; they smoke and drink whiskey.

If someone were to bore a hole into your head and write your dreams down, you would accept them all as the carefully-planned elements of a narration, not of reality. The sky would take its place in the firmament. The stars, the distance, the mathematical meanings.

If no one else will, why not you?

You'd like. You've dozed off, and in the world of dreams people communicate with a few basic words: *unfortunately, if only, because, I'd like.* That's how the party starts, the traffic jam in the streets. The dust. The rain. The firefly hunt.

You've invited everyone you ever loved—and they come without an "I don't know," a "We'll see," or a "Maybe next time." They slide into your head down a chute of otherworldly light. Christina brings you the porcelain cat, its pieces perfectly glued back together. "Stella," she says, "don't overdo it, okay?" And here's Dad, drinking his vodka and scattering cigarette ash everywhere, with the grace of an elephant. Mom gets up out of her wheelchair and tries her new pointe shoes. You're the Holy Family. A dance troupe, starring in *Sleep Lake.*

In that immeasurably vast expanse, the four of you touch the stars and they don't burn you because your own heat is hotter than anything in nature, hotter than anything that has yet been discovered by man. Your heat could burn fire itself.

A Clarification of What I'd Like

My original objective was to write a few short stories to supplement the twenty or so I've published here and there in the past few years. When I started to write, the old stories didn't fit in anywhere—they scurried back to the anthologies they'd come from. So a new objective took shape: to write stories that would read like versions of an unwritten novel. Or, better, to write the biography of those stories as well as of their fictional writer.

All of the stories were written in Berlin. I lived there for a year and a half, but rarely left the house. I listened to the rain. And as often happens in damp climates, I felt my bones creak.

I thank DAAD and the Onassis Foundation for their generous fellowships. I thank Dimitris, Manolis, Soti, and Birgit for reading early drafts. Nina and Anna for their support in the mornings. And my family for their love, patience, and cooking.

A.M.
Berlin, March 2005

SELECTED DALKEY ARCHIVE PAPERBACKS

Petros Abatzoglou, *What Does Mrs. Freeman Want?*
Pierre Albert-Birot, *Grabinoulor.*
Yuz Aleshkovsky, *Kangaroo.*
Felipe Alfau, *Chromos.*
Locos.
Ivan Ângelo, *The Celebration.*
The Tower of Glass.
David Antin, *Talking.*
António Lobo Antunes, *Knowledge of Hell.*
Alain Arias-Misson, *Theatre of Incest.*
Djuna Barnes, *Ladies Almanack.*
Ryder.
John Barth, *LETTERS.*
Sabbatical.
Donald Barthelme, *The King.*
Paradise.
Svetislav Basara, *Chinese Letter.*
Mark Binelli, *Sacco and Vanzetti Must Die!*
Andrei Bitov, *Pushkin House.*
Louis Paul Boon, *Chapel Road.*
Summer in Termuren.
Roger Boylan, *Killoyle.*
Ignácio de Loyola Brandão, *Teeth under the Sun.*
Zero.
Bonnie Bremser, *Troia: Mexican Memoirs.*
Christine Brooke-Rose, *Amalgamemnon.*
Brigid Brophy, *In Transit.*
Meredith Brosnan, *Mr. Dynamite.*
Gerald L. Bruns,
Modern Poetry and the Idea of Language.
Evgeny Bunimovich and J. Kates, eds.,
Contemporary Russian Poetry: An Anthology.
Gabrielle Burton, *Heartbreak Hotel.*
Michel Butor, *Degrees.*
Mobile.
Portrait of the Artist as a Young Ape.
G. Cabrera Infante, *Infante's Inferno.*
Three Trapped Tigers.
Julieta Campos, *The Fear of Losing Eurydice.*
Anne Carson, *Eros the Bittersweet.*
Camilo José Cela, *Christ versus Arizona.*
The Family of Pascual Duarte.
The Hive.
Louis-Ferdinand Céline, *Castle to Castle.*
Conversations with Professor Y.
London Bridge.
North.
Rigadoon.
Hugo Charteris, *The Tide Is Right.*
Jerome Charyn, *The Tar Baby.*
Marc Cholodenko, *Mordechai Schamz.*
Emily Holmes Coleman, *The Shutter of Snow.*
Robert Coover, *A Night at the Movies.*
Stanley Crawford, *Some Instructions to My Wife.*
Robert Creeley, *Collected Prose.*
René Crevel, *Putting My Foot in It.*
Ralph Cusack, *Cadenza.*
Susan Daitch, *L.C.*
Storytown.
Nicholas Delbanco, *The Count of Concord.*
Nigel Dennis, *Cards of Identity.*
Peter Dimock,
A Short Rhetoric for Leaving the Family.
Ariel Dorfman, *Konfidenz.*
Coleman Dowell, *The Houses of Children.*
Island People.
Too Much Flesh and Jabez.
Rikki Ducornet, *The Complete Butcher's Tales.*
The Fountains of Neptune.
The Jade Cabinet.
Phosphor in Dreamland.
The Stain.
The Word "Desire."
William Eastlake, *The Bamboo Bed.*
Castle Keep.
Lyric of the Circle Heart.
Jean Echenoz, *Chopin's Move.*
Stanley Elkin, *A Bad Man.*
Boswell: A Modern Comedy.
Criers and Kibitzers, Kibitzers and Criers.
The Dick Gibson Show.
The Franchiser.
George Mills.
The Living End.
The MacGuffin.
The Magic Kingdom.
Mrs. Ted Bliss.
The Rabbi of Lud.
Van Gogh's Room at Arles.
Annie Ernaux, *Cleaned Out.*
Lauren Fairbanks, *Muzzle Thyself.*
Sister Carrie.
Leslie A. Fiedler,
Love and Death in the American Novel.
Gustave Flaubert, *Bouvard and Pécuchet.*
Ford Madox Ford, *The March of Literature.*
Jon Fosse, *Melancholy.*
Max Frisch, *I'm Not Stiller.*
Man in the Holocene.
Carlos Fuentes, *Christopher Unborn.*
Distant Relations.
Terra Nostra.
Where the Air Is Clear.
Janice Galloway, *Foreign Parts.*
The Trick Is to Keep Breathing.
William H. Gass, *A Temple of Texts.*
The Tunnel.
Willie Masters' Lonesome Wife.
Etienne Gilson, *The Arts of the Beautiful.*
Forms and Substances in the Arts.
C. S. Giscombe, *Giscome Road.*
Here.
Douglas Glover, *Bad News of the Heart.*
The Enamoured Knight.
Witold Gombrowicz, *A Kind of Testament.*
Karen Elizabeth Gordon, *The Red Shoes.*
Georgi Gospodinov, *Natural Novel.*
Juan Goytisolo, *Count Julian.*
Makbara.
Marks of Identity.
Patrick Grainville, *The Cave of Heaven.*
Henry Green, *Blindness.*
Concluding.
Doting.
Nothing.
Jiří Gruša, *The Questionnaire.*
Gabriel Gudding, *Rhode Island Notebook.*
John Hawkes, *Whistlejacket.*
Aidan Higgins, *A Bestiary.*
Bornholm Night-Ferry.
Flotsam and Jetsam.
Langrishe, Go Down.
Scenes from a Receding Past.
Windy Arbours.
Aldous Huxley, *Antic Hay.*
Crome Yellow.
Point Counter Point.
Those Barren Leaves.
Time Must Have a Stop.
Mikhail Iossel and Jeff Parker, eds., *Amerika: Contemporary Russians View the United States.*
Gert Jonke, *Geometric Regional Novel.*
Jacques Jouet, *Mountain R.*
Hugh Kenner, *The Counterfeiters.*
Flaubert, Joyce and Beckett: The Stoic Comedians.
Joyce's Voices.
Danilo Kiš, *Garden, Ashes.*
A Tomb for Boris Davidovich.
Anita Konkka, *A Fool's Paradise.*
George Konrád, *The City Builder.*
Tadeusz Konwicki, *A Minor Apocalypse.*
The Polish Complex.
Menis Koumandareas, *Koula.*
Elaine Kraf, *The Princess of 72nd Street.*
Jim Krusoe, *Iceland.*
Ewa Kuryluk, *Century 21.*
Violette Leduc, *La Bâtarde.*
Deborah Levy, *Billy and Girl.*
Pillow Talk in Europe and Other Places.
José Lezama Lima, *Paradiso.*
Rosa Liksom, *Dark Paradise.*
Osman Lins, *Avalovara.*
The Queen of the Prisons of Greece.
Alf Mac Lochlainn, *The Corpus in the Library.*
Out of Focus.
Ron Loewinsohn, *Magnetic Field(s).*
D. Keith Mano, *Take Five.*
Ben Marcus, *The Age of Wire and String.*
Wallace Markfield, *Teitlebaum's Window.*
To an Early Grave.
David Markson, *Reader's Block.*
Springer's Progress.
Wittgenstein's Mistress.
Carole Maso, *AVA.*
Ladislav Matejka and Krystyna Pomorska, eds.,
Readings in Russian Poetics: Formalist and Structuralist Views.

FOR A FULL LIST OF PUBLICATIONS, VISIT:
www.dalkeyarchive.com

SELECTED DALKEY ARCHIVE PAPERBACKS

Harry Mathews,
The Case of the Persevering Maltese: Collected Essays.
Cigarettes.
The Conversions.
The Human Country: New and Collected Stories.
The Journalist.
My Life in CIA.
Singular Pleasures.
The Sinking of the Odradek Stadium.
Tlooth.
20 Lines a Day.
Robert L. McLaughlin, ed.,
Innovations: An Anthology of Modern & Contemporary Fiction.
Herman Melville, *The Confidence-Man.*
Amanda Michalopoulou, *I'd Like.*
Steven Millhauser, *The Barnum Museum.*
In the Penny Arcade.
Ralph J. Mills, Jr., *Essays on Poetry.*
Olive Moore, *Spleen.*
Nicholas Mosley, *Accident.*
Assassins.
Catastrophe Practice.
Children of Darkness and Light.
Experience and Religion.
The Hesperides Tree.
Hopeful Monsters.
Imago Bird.
Impossible Object.
Inventing God.
Judith.
Look at the Dark.
Natalie Natalia.
Serpent.
Time at War.
The Uses of Slime Mould: Essays of Four Decades.
Warren F. Motte, Jr.,
Fables of the Novel: French Fiction since 1990.
Fiction Now: The French Novel in the 21st Century.
Oulipo: A Primer of Potential Literature.
Yves Navarre, *Our Share of Time.*
Sweet Tooth.
Dorothy Nelson, *In Night's City.*
Tar and Feathers.
Wilfrido D. Nolledo, *But for the Lovers.*
Flann O'Brien, *At Swim-Two-Birds.*
At War.
The Best of Myles.
The Dalkey Archive.
Further Cuttings.
The Hard Life.
The Poor Mouth.
The Third Policeman.
Claude Ollier, *The Mise-en-Scène.*
Patrik Ouředník, *Europeana.*
Fernando del Paso, *Palinuro of Mexico.*
Robert Pinget, *The Inquisitory.*
Mahu or The Material.
Trio.
Raymond Queneau, *The Last Days.*
Odile.
Pierrot Mon Ami.
Saint Glinglin.
Ann Quin, *Berg.*
Passages.
Three.
Tripticks.
Ishmael Reed, *The Free-Lance Pallbearers.*
The Last Days of Louisiana Red.
Reckless Eyeballing.
The Terrible Threes.
The Terrible Twos.
Yellow Back Radio Broke-Down.
Jean Ricardou, *Place Names.*
Julián Ríos, *Larva: A Midsummer Night's Babel.*
Poundemonium.
Augusto Roa Bastos, *I the Supreme.*
Olivier Rolin, *Hotel Crystal.*
Jacques Roubaud, *The Great Fire of London.*
Hortense in Exile.
Hortense Is Abducted.
The Plurality of Worlds of Lewis.
The Princess Hoppy.
The Form of a City Changes Faster, Alas, Than the Human Heart.
Some Thing Black.
Leon S. Roudiez, *French Fiction Revisited.*
Vedrana Rudan, *Night.*
Lydie Salvayre, *The Company of Ghosts.*
Everyday Life.
The Lecture.
The Power of Flies.
Luis Rafael Sánchez, *Macho Camacho's Beat.*
Severo Sarduy, *Cobra & Maitreya.*
Nathalie Sarraute, *Do You Hear Them?*
Martereau.
The Planetarium.
Arno Schmidt, *Collected Stories.*
Nobodaddy's Children.
Christine Schutt, *Nightwork.*
Gail Scott, *My Paris.*
June Akers Seese,
Is This What Other Women Feel Too?
What Waiting Really Means.
Aurelie Sheehan, *Jack Kerouac Is Pregnant.*
Viktor Shklovsky, *Knight's Move.*
A Sentimental Journey: Memoirs 1917-1922.
Energy of Delusion: A Book on Plot.
Literature and Cinematography.
Theory of Prose.
Third Factory.
Zoo, or Letters Not about Love.
Josef Škvorecký,
The Engineer of Human Souls.
Claude Simon, *The Invitation.*
Gilbert Sorrentino, *Aberration of Starlight.*
Blue Pastoral.
Crystal Vision.
Imaginative Qualities of Actual Things.
Mulligan Stew.
Pack of Lies.
Red the Fiend.
The Sky Changes.
Something Said.
Splendide-Hôtel.
Steelwork.
Under the Shadow.
W. M. Spackman, *The Complete Fiction.*
Gertrude Stein, *Lucy Church Amiably.*
The Making of Americans.
A Novel of Thank You.
Piotr Szewc, *Annihilation.*
Stefan Themerson, *Hobson's Island.*
The Mystery of the Sardine.
Tom Harris.
Jean-Philippe Toussaint, *Monsieur.*
Television.
Dumitru Tsepeneag, *Vain Art of the Fugue.*
Esther Tusquets, *Stranded.*
Dubravka Ugresic, *Lend Me Your Character.*
Thank You for Not Reading.
Mati Unt, *Diary of a Blood Donor.*
Things in the Night.
Eloy Urroz, *The Obstacles.*
Luisa Valenzuela, *He Who Searches.*
Paul Verhaeghen, *Omega Minor.*
Marja-Liisa Vartio, *The Parson's Widow.*
Boris Vian, *Heartsnatcher.*
Austryn Wainhouse, *Hedyphagetica.*
Paul West, *Words for a Deaf Daughter & Gala.*
Curtis White, *America's Magic Mountain.*
The Idea of Home.
Memories of My Father Watching TV.
Monstrous Possibility: An Invitation to Literary Politics.
Requiem.
Diane Williams, *Excitability: Selected Stories.*
Romancer Erector.
Douglas Woolf, *Wall to Wall.*
Ya! & John-Juan.
Jay Wright, *Polynomials and Pollen.*
The Presentable Art of Reading Absence.
Philip Wylie, *Generation of Vipers.*
Marguerite Young, *Angel in the Forest.*
Miss MacIntosh, My Darling.
REYoung, *Unbabbling.*
Zoran Živković, *Hidden Camera.*
Louis Zukofsky, *Collected Fiction.*
Scott Zwiren, *God Head.*